The Rocker That Holds Her

Terri Anne Browning

Other Books By Terri Anne Browning

Reese: A Safe Haven Novella

Reckless With Their Hearts (Duet with Anna Howard)

Books In This Series

The Rocker That Holds Me

The Rocker That Savors Me

The Rocker That Needs Me

The Rocker That Loves Me

Copyrights

The Rocker That Holds Her

Written By Terri Anne Browning

Edited By Maxann Dobson. The Polished Pen

All Rights Reserved © Anna Henson 2013

ISBN-13: 978-1494233556

ISBN-10: 149423355X

This is a work of fiction. Any characters, names, places or incidents are used solely in a fictitious nature based on the author's imagination. Any resemblance to or mention of persons, place, organizations, or other incidents are completely coincidental. No part of this book may be reproduced or transmitted in any form or by any other means without permission from the Publisher. Piracy is not a victimless crime. No individual/group has resale rights, sharing rights, or any other kind of rights to sell or give away this book. This is the author's livelihood. Please respect her rights.

Acknowledgements

The last year has been a journey in and of itself. *The Rocker That Holds Me* came out at the end of January and since then my life has become the one that I could only ever dream about. I have so many people that I need to thank and show appreciation to. My husband, always the center of my universe and the reason I can do this amazing job without worrying about the outside world intruding. Thanks for putting up with me and my crazy mood swings as I put my heart and soul into all of the Demons. My BETAs who have guided me through the maze of creating all of the Demons. Neda, Amanda, Donna, Maureen, Holly, and Nikki—I would be so lost without you! And of course my lovely editor Max, for polishing my work until it shines. Thank you all for sticking by me while I chase my rainbows.

Dedication

To the fans! Because you f*ing ROCK!

The Rocker That Holds Her

Table of Contents

Chapter 1
Chapter 2
Chapter 3
Chapter 4
Chapter 5
Chapter 6
Chapter 7
Chapter 8
Chapter 9
Chapter 10
Chapter 11
Chapter 12
Chapter 13
Chapter 14
Chapter 15
Chapter 16
Chapter 17
Chapter 18
Chapter 19
Chapter 20
Epilogue

The Rocker That Holds Her

Chapter 1

Meeting Emmie

I'm not sure what made me look out the window.

Mom was in the kitchen washing dishes, making sure that the place was her standard of clean before sitting down. It was a nice change to the way my old man had kept the place before he died a few years back. Back then it had smelled like stale smoke, beer, and at times the old bastard's own waste. Now it smelled like sweet pine and some kind of floral spray that Mom couldn't seem to leave the grocery store without.

I was lying on my bed just glaring up at the ceiling. My best friends weren't home this weekend. Jesse's dad had dragged him to some poker game across the bridge in Huntington, West Virginia, and they wouldn't be back until the next day. Drake and Shane were on a camping trip with their mom and stepdad since their mother had the weekend off. Meanwhile, I was stuck here.

I hated it here. Hated this rundown trailer, in this rundown trailer park, in Nowhere, Ohio. Maybe it was the memories of my dad and birth mother. Of being beaten in the middle of the night for no reason. My Mom, who was really just my aunt, had been my saving grace when the old fucker died. She had given up her life and moved into this crappy trailer to take care of me.

For that I would always be grateful. Which was why I wanted out of Ohio. When I got out of Ohio, I would make it big. I knew I would. Drake and I were crazy good at music. We could get a record deal, and I would be able to take care of my mom the way she deserved to be taken care of.

Big dreams for a small town boy with nothing more than a passion for singing and playing around in the band room at school, but it was all I had. I was determined that it was all I would need.

I sat up, not sure if I wanted to go into the living room and watch some television, or maybe go across the trailer park and see if I could talk Missy Snuffer into taking a walk down by the train tracks with me. It wouldn't be the first time I had asked, and it wouldn't be the first time I would attempt—and more than likely succeed—in getting to second base with the sixteen-year-old.

Before I could make up my mind, my gaze caught something outside of my bedroom window, and for some reason I felt like I was sucker punched in the gut. There, on the grass that separated my trailer from the one next door, sat a little bundle of rags. At least at first glance it looked like rags. Moving closer to the window, I saw that it was a little girl, maybe four but no more than five. Her hair was a mess, tangled and dirty, but that didn't disguise the pretty auburn color. Her clothes were old and tattered. There was a hole in the knee of her leggings and a bleach stain on her pink shirt.

The little girl's face was dirty and streaked with tears. She looked lost and sad as she held on tight to a teddy bear that I couldn't tell if it looked better or worse than the girl. It was raggedy, missing its right eye, and its left ear was just hanging on by a thread. I was transfixed as the little girl rocked the teddy bear and whispered to it like it was her only friend in the world. My chest ached just watching her.

The Rocker That Holds Her

I was walking through the trailer before I even realized my feet were moving. Mom raised an eyebrow at me when I opened the freezer and pulled out two Popsicles. Instead of answering her unspoken question, I just kissed her cheek and headed outside. The little girl hadn't moved. Relief filled me seeing her still sitting on the grass by my window.

The sound of my shoes crunching on a few rocks caused the girl's head to lift, and big green eyes snapped up at me. She looked frightened, nervous. I took a few steps toward her and could see that she was pale under her dirty face and had to hide my frown the closer I got.

"Hey," I greeted her. I hadn't dealt with many young kids, so I wasn't sure how to approach her.

She looked hesitantly at me, those big eyes of hers pulling at something in my chest in a way that was almost painful. "Hi," she whispered softly, her grip on the nasty old bear tightening.

I opened up one of the Popsicles—cherry, my favorite. "It's hot out here. Want something cold to eat?"

Her gaze went to the already melting Popsicle and she licked her lips, but she hesitated. I thought that was incredibly smart for a kid her age. "I ..."

I took a few steps closer and sat down on the dry grass beside her. "Here, it's good. Cherry is the best flavor in the box."

Little fingers latched onto the stick, and I noticed that they trembled a little as she took the cold treat from me. As she lifted the Popsicle to her lips, I saw the first bruise. It was big, or maybe it was just because her arms were so little it looked big. The bruise was all kinds of colors starting with dark blue on the outside and ending with a yellow-green in the middle. It looked like it still hurt, even though it had to be at least a week old.

I could tell how old the bruise was easily enough. I had spent years with those same bruises all over my body. My dad wasn't happy unless he was beating on me. My birth mother had sat back and let him have his fun. For a while, even after she had killed herself, I had thought she enjoyed watching her only kid being smacked around for sport. It wasn't until her sister—the woman I felt was my true mother—had come into my life that I had realized that my birth mother had probably just been happy that the old bastard wasn't using her as the punching bag.

"My name is Nik," I told the girl, feeling sick as thoughts of her being hit like I once had been filled my mind. "What's yours?"

"E-ember."

"That's a cool name." I smiled, trying to let her see that I was harmless. I would never hurt anyone the way I had been hurt, especially this little baby. "How old are you?"

She held up her left hand. "Five," she said before biting into the Popsicle.

"I'm fifteen." I opened the second Popsicle and bit it in half. Orange wasn't my favorite, but it would do. "When did you move in?" I hadn't seen her before, and the trailer beside mine hadn't been rented out in a while. I could hear movement inside the beat up home on wheels, so assumed her parents were in there.

"This mornin'." She took another big bite of the sweet treat. "We used to live in West Virginia, but Momma said we had to move."

I couldn't help but smile at her country accent. One more bite and the snack was gone. When her gaze went to my half-finished Popsicle, I quickly offered it over. "Here, take it." I wiped my sticky fingers on my jeans. "I don't want it anyway," I lied.

Midnight Caller

I wasn't asleep.

How could I knowing that she was in that trailer? With that bitch? That *monster*? I hated Emmie's mother at first sight: the way she had smelled of smoke and booze and something more sour; the glassiness in her eyes; the stagger in her step; and her tone she took with Emmie when she had seen the little girl talking with me.

"Get in the trailer, girl. Clean your room, before I …" She hadn't finished the threat, but Emmie had been trembling ever so slightly before going into the trailer, and her mother slammed the old storm door behind her.

I wanted to bundle Emmie up then and there and bring her home with me—protect her, feed her, take care of the little baby doll that she was—but I knew that I couldn't. My mom wouldn't understand, and I wasn't sure if I should tell her or anyone else what I suspected—knew!—was going on with our new neighbors. I had been taken away from my parents once, when the bruises were too many to count and hard to explain away. I knew what the homes were like. Foster parents could be just as bad as real parents.

And a pretty little girl like Emmie?

I shuddered and pulled the covers up over my stomach. My eyes closed and I started to drift off...

A *tap, tap, tap* at my window made my eyes snap open. Earlier I had told Emmie if she needed me, day or night, to knock on my bedroom window. I had even shown her how to do it. I'd told her it was our secret when she looked lost and more than a little frightened after her mother had gone back inside.

Heart pounding, I jumped up from my bed and peeked through my window. Emmie was standing on the bucket I had set up for her. I couldn't make out more than the outline of her thin little body in the darkness, but I knew it was her. Quietly, I lowered the window and reached out to help her inside.

By the light of my old television set, I saw that she was bleeding. There was a little cut on her cheek and a few more on her arms that I could see. Tears poured down that baby doll face, and I felt my eyes burn with some of my own. "What happened?" I whispered.

"I wanted a glass of water...but one of her friends was over..." she broke off with a shrug that made her seem much older than just five years old.

I didn't ask any more questions for the moment. Instead, I went into my bathroom and grabbed a box of Band-Aids and the ointment that Mom always put on my scratches. As I cleaned her cuts, I realized that they were from a switch and had started welting up. My hatred for the woman grew, and I was daydreaming of how I would torture that bitch as I cleaned Emmie up.

"Ouch!" Emmie whimpered as I put a little dab of the ointment on the cut on her face.

"Sorry, baby doll," I whispered, "but these could get infected." It was what my mom always told me when I was being a big baby and didn't want the stingy ointment. "Do you want to have to go to the doctor and get a shot if they get infected?"

Emmie bit her lip but shook her head. She was quiet for the next few minutes while I finished taking care of her cuts. Every time she whimpered from the sting, I felt tears burn my eyes a little more and had to keep blinking before I embarrassed myself by crying in front of this little girl. She was so strong, so brave.

After using nearly half the box of Band-Aids, I put her in my twin bed and tucked the covers around her. "You can sleep here tonight, but you have to go home before my mom wakes up," I explained to her. "If she finds you here she will call the cops, Emmie."

She just nodded and laid her head on my extra pillow. I took my favorite pillow and an old quilt and camped out on the floor while she slept, but sleep was not my friend that night. I watched over my new little treasure, this little baby doll that had come to me when I had needed someone the most. She was sent to me so I could protect her, and I would.

I must have fallen asleep. When I woke up it was morning and Emmie was gone. I went to the window to see if she was outside. She wasn't, but there in the window of her trailer I could see her looking out, as if watching for me. That ragged old bear once more clenched in her arms.

Chapter 2

Record Deal

Sweat was pouring down my back. My face and hair felt like I had dunked it in a bucket of water it was so drenched with it. I always gave each performance a hundred and ten percent no matter where we were playing. Lately we had been doing more and more bars. The owners loved it when Demon's Wings did a live set for them. We always brought in a crowd for them, and more often than not they would end up having to turn people away, or put a bouncer at the door to make sure that the place didn't get a fine from the fire marshal for being over capacity.

I used the towel Drake tossed at me and wiped my face. I was exhausted. Not only was this my night gig, but I was working day shift to help out my mom now that she had been diagnosed with early Alzheimer's. The last doctor's visit hadn't been a good one, and he was even talking about assisted living in the near future. I knew he was right on some level but hated to think that the woman who had dedicated her life to making mine better was losing her mind.

A strong hand landed on my shoulder. Jesse slapped me on the back, and I grunted under the force. "Good set, bro."

I could only nod my thanks as I downed a bottle of water. My throat was a little sore, and I didn't want to waste what little voice I still had by talking just yet.

"You boys have a gift!"

The voice was one I didn't recognize, and I raised my head to find a guy in a suit standing on the steps that led backstage. He looked like a dick, but he also looked like my salvation. I knew who he was, had heard through the vine that a rock manager was looking for some new talent to pimp. Rich Branson had signed the hottest rock band on the radio just a year or so ago with OtherWorld.

Three beers and a bunch of handshakes later we had a deal—a shitload of money and the life I had always dreamed of was offered to me and my three best friends. I wouldn't have to bust my ass to pay for the bills and the treatment my mom needed.

It also meant that we were leaving in a week and we couldn't take Emmie with us. We all knew that with the money we were being offered we could easily take care of Emmie. Send her money, get her the things she needed that her mother didn't ever supply, but we couldn't exactly take care of her from California. And that was exactly where we were headed.

We all got wasted that night as guilt for what we were about to do churned in our guts.

Saying Goodbye

I couldn't even look at her as all of us stood in the yard that separated my trailer from Emmie's.

I knew this was going to be hard, but I never, ever imagined it would be like this! We had been busy making arrangements all week: making sure that Emmie had enough money and that it was hidden from her mother; getting her a phone so she could talk to us every day; finding the right person that was trustworthy and paying them out the ass to make sure that Emmie was okay while we were so far away.

Drake and Shane had already said their good-byes. Each had hugged her hard and long, telling her that they loved her and would talk to her soon. Now Jesse had her in his arms, rocking her as she sobbed into his chest. Each shake of her body was like a twist of a dagger in my chest. I hadn't seen my little baby doll cry in years, so those tears and broken sobs made direct hits to my heart.

Jesse was having a hard time controlling his own tears. He was more protective of Emmie than even I was. One look at her baby doll face and he had been helpless as she wrapped herself around his heart. "I'll call you every night," Jesse promised again, for what had to be the hundredth time that morning. "If you need me I'll be on the first plane back."

Emmie just nodded her auburn head, unable to speak through her sobs.

He held on a few minutes more. Finally, he unwrapped her from the tangled hold she had on him. With a tortured look, he kissed her forehead and turned away, not allowing Emmie to see the tears streaming down his face.

My little baby doll just stood there, shoulders trembling as she watched Jesse walk away through her tears. Emmie had grown up a lot in the six years since I had first met her. She might only be eleven now, but she had an old soul. After living the life she had, seeing things that no human being should ever have to see—let alone a child—she was beyond mature for her age.

I wasn't as strong as my friends. I knew that as soon as I hugged her I wasn't going to be able to get on the plane.

Instead, I kissed her cheek and whispered, "Bye, baby doll," before following Jesse.

My heart broke in my chest when her sobs stopped. I knew then that not hugging her good-bye had been a mistake. I knew that she thought I was abandoning her, but there was nothing I could do about it. In that moment I was worried more about my sanity than her hurt feelings.

The next weeks were busy. I had meetings with the record labels to sign contracts and start my rocker life. On top of that I was looking for the best assisted living facility that money could pay for. I wanted my mom on the West Coast with me so I could keep an eye on her in between the tours that Rich Branson had already committed us to.

Each night after dinner the guys and I would call Emmie. She talked and talked and talked to Drake, Shane, and Jesse. But when it was my turn to chat I got cold, monosyllable answers. Was school going well? *Yes.* Was her mom treating her ok? *Yes.* Did she need anything? *No.* I felt like I was being stabbed repeatedly each night. When I found out that she was calling the others several times a day, it was another stab to the heart. The few times I had tried to call her in the middle of the day, I had only gotten her voice mail.

By the time our first tour started I had things with my mom sorted out. She was living at one of the best facilities in the country and she seemed happy there. Her condition had seemed to worsen since we had gotten to California, and there were days that she didn't even recognize me when I went to visit her.

Stressed out, feeling heartbroken over my mom and the way Emmie was treating me, I started drinking. Not as much as Drake, but I was catching up. I felt angry all the time, lost and lonely more often than not. This was the life I had always wanted. The rock 'n' roll lifestyle that I had dreamed about for so long. I had a huge bank account, girls dropping their panties for me every night, fame, and best of all people were listening to *my* music.

So why wasn't I happy?

Going Home

"Good night, Cleveland!"

I tried not to roll my eyes as Axton Cage stepped off the stage with a handful of roses, and even more panties.

For the last three months we had been touring with OtherWorld. We were both headliners, and with each new city, we switched who would end the show. Since Cleveland was so close to our hometown, we were closing it out tonight. Of course that didn't stop Axton and me from betting who could get the best reaction from the crowd.

I had to give it to the man, he could rock hard. But I knew I was better, knew that I would get the crowd going more than he had. He stopped beside me as he left the stage, a bottle of water in his free hand, twirling a lacy black thong on his index finger. "Top that, fucker."

The thing about Axton was you either liked him or hated him. There was no in between with him. Lucky for him I happened to like the jerk, otherwise I might have already put my fist in his face and made him swallow some of those pearly whites in that perfect smile of his. But sharing one tour bus between the two bands on this tour had left us all as friends in the short time we had been on the road together.

So I grinned at my new friend. "Oh, I plan on it."

Axton dropped his pile of flowers and underwear and opened his water. "Yeah, I figured you would." He stood with me while the stage was turned from an OtherWorld wonderland to a Demon's Wings nightmare theme. "There are a few hot ones in the front row. Maybe you'll see something you like."

I gritted my teeth. "Yeah, maybe." But I doubted it. In the year since Demon's Wings had left Ohio for the bright lights of California, I had grown tired of all the girls throwing themselves at me. I hated to admit it to anyone, myself included, but I was tired of this life I had dreamed of for most of my life.

Maybe it had something to do with not having Emmie in my life at the moment. The little baby doll that had been a huge part of my world wasn't even speaking to me these days. I had hated the monosyllable conversations that we first had when I had moved away. Now I actually wished that I could even get that much out of her. I had to rely on Jesse, Drake, and Shane to fill me in on what was happening with her.

I was hoping when we went to visit her the next morning I could get her to forgive me. That she would see things from my point and understand why I hadn't given her a proper good-bye all those months ago.

Halfway through our set I had the crowd chanting our name. I was in my element. The stage was littered with broken red roses, bras that had girls' names and numbers on the inside cups, and panties. I had to admit that as tired as I was from all the other crap, I knew that I would never get bored with this. I loved performing for a live crowd, loved the reaction of the fans. Got high from the adrenaline rush it gave me.

My full attention was given to the song I was singing. Winking, blowing kisses to the girls in the front row that kept throwing me roses as I sang. Rinse and repeat. I saw nothing beyond that. So when Jesse suddenly stopped drumming right in the middle of our last song I nearly stumbled on the words.

Drake left me next, the guitar solo never coming, and I turned around to find that both he and Shane were running across the stage and heading straight for the crowd. Jesse was already in the masses, pushing his way through the now screaming fans as they tried to get to him. "Get the fuck off!" he bellowed and then he was on his knees.

That was when I saw her: thin little arms holding onto the big bald man; auburn hair flying back as Jesse stood with her in his arms; a dirty, tear stained, baby doll face.

The fans were going crazy, screaming for the guys to take the stage and finish the concert. Jesse didn't respond to the group of guys standing close to him and cursing. Shane and Drake had reached Jesse now. They pushed two loud guys back when they tried to charge at Jesse.

I tossed my microphone away, no longer caring about finishing the set. Screw the crowd. All I wanted was to hold Emmie and find out if she was okay. Jumping down from the stage I pushed my way through a group of girls who screamed and tried to get hold of my shirt as I passed. The material tore, leaving a hole at the hem. Hands touched my face, their nails leaving scratches.

I snarled something unintelligible at the bitch who stood between me and the only girl that could ever touch my heart. The skank stepped back, as if I was about to hit her, and really I couldn't be sure if I wouldn't have.

Jesse turned to face me, his eyes wild, and I knew that something wasn't right. I took Emmie from him, knowing that I was risking life and limb by doing so but not giving a fuck for either. All I wanted was to hold Emmie!

She stiffened in my arms. Big green eyes glared up at me, and I tried to tell her everything I couldn't with my eyes as I tightened my hold on her. Our gazes locked for a moment in a battle of wills, one I prayed I would win.

My heart melted when she threw her little arms around my neck and sobbed. "Nik!"

I sighed, sure that I had been offered a pardon for all my crimes in her eyes, as I carried her away from the craziness of the crowd. Drake and Shane kept a path clear as Jesse brought up the rear, making sure that any disgruntled fans didn't try to get to me and the precious bundle in my arms.

Axton and Rich were waiting on us when we reached backstage. Rich was spitting he was in such a rage. Axton just looked concerned. "What the hell, man? Is she okay?"

"Shut the fuck up!" Jesse told Rich when he demanded we go back out on stage. "Get out of the way or I will move you."

I combed my fingers through Emmie's tangled hair, tried not to gag at the way the strands smelled of booze, smoke, and something else. "Just find me somewhere that we won't be bothered."

"Is she your sister or something?" Axton asked as he led the way down a narrow hall, searching random rooms for a place we could take Emmie.

"Or something," Shane muttered.

Finally we found a room with a couch. I pushed past Axton and sat with Emmie still clinging to my neck. Her sobs were shaking us both and it broke my heart. I grasped her shoulders and pulled her back enough so I could inspect her for any damage.

Her face was unharmed, except for the tear stains down her cheeks, but there were bruises on her neck, as if someone had tried to choke her. She was holding her arm a little awkwardly and I grasped it. She whimpered in pain as my fingers skimmed over her swollen wrist.

"I think it's broken," I said quietly, trying not to frighten her.

Jesse muttered a curse. Shane left to find ice while I continued to examine Emmie, but other than the usual bruises, I couldn't see that anything else was wrong. "What happened, Emmie? How did you even get here?" I asked quietly.

"I heard on the radio that you were going to be in Cleveland. I wanted to come see you guys, but Momma was high when I asked her... She pushed me against the wall and started choking me. I tried to push her off and she grabbed my wrist." Her chin trembled. "I hitchhiked ..."

"You did what?!" Jesse exploded, only to grimace when she flinched at his harsh tone. "Emmie, do you realize how dangerous that was?"

Chin still trembling, she nodded her head. "I'm sorry," she whispered.

"Her mother did this?" Axton exclaimed, and I realized for the first time that he was still with us. Drake motioned him to the back of the room and started talking to him in hushed tones so Emmie couldn't hear them.

"Here we go, sweetheart." Shane had a bag of ice and a bottle of Tylenol in his hands. "Let's get you feeling better."

She gave him a watery smile as she swallowed the tablets and put on a brave face as he placed the ice on her injured wrist.

"We have to go to the hospital, Emmie." I combed my fingers through her tangled hair, trying to keep her calm even though I knew that even mentioning a visit to the hospital would do anything but.

Big green eyes widened in horror. "No. No, please no."

"I'm sorry, baby doll. But if your wrist is broken it will have to be set." I glanced at Jesse for help when she started sobbing again.

He crouched down beside me, taking Emmie's good hand into his. "You have to be brave now, Emmie. No tears. A broken wrist is serious." Emmie sucked in a few breaths, trying to stop the broken sobs. "I'll be right there holding your hand while the doctors fix you up. Okay?"

"P-promise?"

"Promise." He lifted her into his arms and carried her to the door, leaving the rest of us to follow.

The Rocker That Holds Her

It was nearly dawn before we got Emmie home. I didn't want her to go, but we all knew that she had to. Jesse held the now sleeping Emmie in his arms, her left wrist in a cast now. I knocked on the door with my three friends standing at my back while we waited for the evil bitch to open the door.

Two minutes passed before she opened the door, nearly stumbling out in her hungover state. Jesse growled something under his breath. I gave the woman a once-over, taking in her almost emaciated figure. Her face was so thin it looked like someone had pulled skin tight over a skeleton. I wasn't sure how old she was, but she looked close to fifty. Her dyed red hair was dry and lifeless, her eyes empty just as her soul was.

"Well look at you boys." She leaned against the door frame, a cigarette hanging from her lips. "What brings the big shot rockers back to this hellhole?"

"We need to talk," I said, grinding my teeth.

A dark brow lifted. "Oh yeah?"

"Yeah." I pushed past her into the disaster of a trailer that Emmie had to live in. There were beer bottles tossed here and there, overflowing ash trays with things much stronger than what she was currently smoking stinking up the air, and even a few needles abandoned on the coffee table in front of the old couch.

Jesse, Drake, and Shane followed me inside. Jesse took Emmie down the hall to put Emmie into bed while we made a deal with the Devil.

Chapter 3

A Deep Sigh Of Relief

I wouldn't say that things got better after our stop in Ohio, but they didn't get any worse.

After setting things up so that Emmie's mother would have plenty of money to keep her drugged out of her mind for the most part—and keep Emmie *off* her mind—Emmie's homelife became a little safer. We all called her several times a day, and I was doing better emotionally since we were now talking like we used to.

Even with the medication, my mom wasn't doing any better. More often than not she didn't know who I was when I went to visit her. But other than the dementia, she didn't look unhealthy. The nurses were taking exceptional care of her and that made me sleep a little easier at night, especially when I was off touring with the guys.

Our name was getting out there. Our second album in three years had gone triple platinum. We were winning music awards and having our songs added to movies and television shows. I was starting to write more and fans were going crazy for my songs. I didn't know I had such a passion for songwriting, but I was pretty talented.

Three years had flown by so quickly. There hadn't been any downtime since our rocker life had started, and we were all feeling the need for a vacation. At the moment we were halfway through a tour with OtherWorld. Of all the bands we had toured with over the last few years OtherWorld was the most interesting.

We had all become friends, but we kind of adopted Axton into our brotherhood. If we were touring with him, he was on our bus more often than his own. OtherWorld wasn't nearly as close as we were. With Demon's Wings, we weren't just bandmates, we were brothers. We had grown up together, seen each other at our lowest, and stuck together through the harshest of times. Jesse, Drake, Shane, and Emmie were my family—all I had in the world now that my mom was checking out in the mind department.

There were three hours to go before Demon's Wings were scheduled to take the stage. I was sitting on the long couch backstage drinking a beer and tossing my phone up and catching it. I was bored out of my fucking mind. Shane was off getting cozy with two girls that had snuck backstage, while his brother was getting cozy with another bottle of Jack Daniels. Who knew where Jesse was, because really it could have been anyone's guess. He could have been getting lost between some girl's legs or off causing trouble with Liam and Zander.

When my phone rang I knew who it was. Knew that she was calling to tell me how her day was. Emmie and high school were not mixing well. For one, she didn't do the whole friend thing with girls. Most of the girls that she went to school with knew that Emmie was under our protection, so they only ever approached her in hopes of getting to approach *us*. And… well… Emmie was strong willed with a temper to match her hair, and a mind that saw everything from every angle.

I was smiling as I hit connect on my cellphone and lifted it to my ears. "Hey, baby doll. How's my favorite girl?"

Instead of jumping into bitching about her day she was quiet. I could feel her tension even over the phone. My stomach bottomed out as I tried to keep all the possibilities out of mind—Emmie hurt, broken, bleeding. If her mother had dared to hurt Emmie again I would tear her apart this time.

"Em?" I croaked out.

"Momma's dead. She overdosed." Her voice was devoid of all emotions. It was like I was talking to a robotic Emmie. "I called the cops, but they said it could take them a while to get the paramedics out here to get the body…"

I was already on my feet, already mentally making a list of what had to be done. "Are you okay? Where are you now?"

"At the trailer… but the cops said social services will be coming to get me soon…"

I started jogging, the urgency to get back to Ohio hitting the red zone now. I couldn't let social services take Emmie. I would never see her again. She would get lost in the system. And only god knew what would happen to her in a foster home. "I'm coming. We will be there by tonight." Even if I had to hire a private jet to get me there I was going to be there that night. "Hide. Do you hear me, Em? Hide. Don't let them take you."

"Okay." She sounded so calm and I figured she was in shock.

I didn't want to but I hung up. I found Jesse and Drake down the corridor hanging with Axton, Liam, and Zander. They were passing a bottle of Jack between them and laughing about something. Zander I liked, while Liam was a hit or miss for me most days. He had a borderline drug problem that I couldn't wrap my head around. Drugs were something I hadn't ever touched and didn't ever plan to.

Emmie's mother's drug use had made her life hell and I wasn't ever going to do that to her.

When Jesse saw me he frowned. "What's with you?"

"Emmie." That was all I had to say and he and Drake were on red alert. "We have to go. Now." I would explain to them on the plane. Right then I had other things to deal with. I looked at Axton. "We're out. Don't know when we can make it back."

"Yeah, sure, man. Go deal with your family. I'll take care of fuck-face Branson."

Finding Shane was easy enough. First bathroom we came to and I could hear the girls moaning. I didn't waste time. Just walked on in. With one on her knees and the other sitting on the edge of the sink with Shane's hands between her legs they were obviously having a good time. "Emmie needs us. Let's go."

Shane pushed the girl on her knees away and stuffed himself back into his jeans. "I'm coming."

"No you aren't," the blonde still on her knees giggled.

"Shut up, bitch," the brunette on the sink told her friend.

It took us four hours to get to Ohio once we got the plane sorted. It was nearly nine-thirty by the time we pulled up in front of the old trailer that belonged to Emmie. There was a cop car sitting in the gravel driveway close to the front door. The trailer was dark but the cop was sitting on the front steps with a woman that had a clipboard in her hands.

I breathed a sigh of relief. They hadn't found Emmie yet.

Jesse started to get out of the backseat of the Cadillac SUV that we had rented at the airport, but I grabbed his arm before he or the others could get out. "Keep a level head. We have to play this right so we can take Emmie with us."

My band brothers nodded, their jaws clenched hard as we all finally got out of the SUV and headed for the social worker and the cop. I was beyond happy that the social worker was a female and young. She wasn't bad to look at, but she wasn't anywhere near beautiful. Her hair was pulled back in a tight bun that made her face look too harsh to be pretty. Her body, while slender, was hidden under unflattering clothes that hung off her body in an unappealing way.

The cop was someone I remembered well. He had been one of the cops that had arrested Drake when he had beaten his sick-ass stepdad unconscious six years before. After Drake and Shane's mother had killed the bastard, the cops let Drake go. The man sitting on Emmie's front steps had even come to Mrs. Nelson's funeral.

Recognizing us, the cop stood. "Boys." Officer Brady nodded his head in greeting. "I figured you would be showing up sooner than later."

I offered the man my hand. "She's ours." It was a simple enough answer, but a true one. Emmie had belonged to us since she was five years old.

"This is Miss Hill. By law she has to take Ember. She's only fifteen and as far as I know there are no living relatives."

I shook my head and pulled out the paper that I had been waiting three years to use. Three years of paying five grand a month to the Devil for this one piece of paper. I would have paid more—double, triple, fuck ten times that amount—each month. Emmie's mother had set that amount and I wasn't going to tell her no. Not when she had given me what I wanted.

I unfolded the simple sheet of paper with the woman's handwriting on it, and more importantly her signature at the bottom, and handed it over to Officer Brady. "She's Jesse's sister."

The man raised an eyebrow at the lie but didn't say anything as he read the paper that we had been smart enough to have notarized. If there had been time I would have made that bitch go one step further and had a lawyer draw up the right legal documents, but there hadn't been time.

"Mr. Thorton, is this true?" Miss Hill asked after reading the notarized sheet of paper in the dim light that came from the cop car's headlights. "You are Ember Jameson's brother?"

Jesse's father had died from a massive stroke just two years ago so there wasn't anyone that could dispute our claim. Unless they wanted a DNA test, but with the notarized letter there was no reason for that. Jesse nodded. "Yes, ma'am. I'm her brother."

The social worker frowned down at the paper then let out a frustrated sigh. "Well, we will have to speak to the notary that signed off on this. But I am sorry to inform you that Ember has run away."

I shrugged. "I'm sure she is just upset about her mother. We know all of Emmie's hiding spots. Finding her won't be a problem … that is if you are letting us have her?"

Cool blue eyes looked right through me. "No. I am not letting *you* have her." My stomach actually twisted into a knot until she turned that cool gaze back to Jesse. "But as her only living relative, I will sign her over into *your* custody, Mr. Thorton, as soon as the notary has authenticated all signatures."

There was no describing the relief I felt. Knowing that Emmie was ours now—okay, Jesse's but whatever—was like having the pressure of the world lifted from my shoulders. The social worker handed Jesse a stack of papers, told him he would have to come down to her office first thing the next morning with Emmie, and left with Officer Brady. I waited until the cop car's taillights had been out of sight for a good ten minutes before calling Emmie's cellphone.

"Nik?"

"Are you hungry?" I suddenly felt as if I were starving. "How about some pizza?"

"I'm not hungry." She sounded tired but there was still no emotion in her voice. I couldn't begin to understand what was wrong with Emmie until I had her warm, fed, and safely tucked into bed back in the hotel I had reserved for us.

"Let's get out of here, baby doll." I glanced at Shane, Drake, and Jesse. They were all looking a little anxious to get out of here. "We're all tired and need a good night's sleep."

"Are the cops gone?"

"All gone, sweetheart," I promised her.

The Rocker That Holds Her

"I can go with you? They aren't going to take me away?" There was a small hitch in her voice this time.

"Ah, Emmie. Do you honestly think we would let them take you from us? No way! You're ours now."

The phone disconnected and at first I thought maybe something had happened to her. "Emmie?" I glanced around, hoping that she had hidden somewhere close by. "Emmie!" I shouted her name when I didn't get an answer.

The others started calling for her too. Drake and Shane headed off to some of her usual hiding spots. Jesse rubbed a hand over his bald head, worry in his eyes. "Em?" He turned in a full circle. "Where are you, Em?"

The sound of tin bending caught my attention, and I had a sense of déjà vu when I saw thin legs crawling out from under her trailer. Only this time Emmie wasn't a beaten little rag doll, hiding from her mother until we could find her and keep her safe. Now she was ours and we were taking her home with us.

Jesse was like lightning. I still couldn't get over how fast and smooth that big man could move. Before Emmie's head could come out from under the trailer he had her in his arms. "Stop, I smell bad," she complained when Jesse held on to her for dear life.

"Don't give a fuck." Jesse laughed as he swung her around and around. "God, Emmie, it's so good to see you again."

I grimaced. We hadn't seen Emmie in person in nearly eighteen months. Texting and phone calls throughout the day didn't show us how she was growing. And she sure as fuck had grown since the last time I had laid eyes on her. She was at least four inches taller, her auburn hair hanging half way down her back. And even in the dim light of a distant streetlamp I could tell that Emmie was no longer my pretty little baby doll.

Fifteen year old Emmie was beautiful!

--

It took us four days to get everything situated with Emmie.

We made sure her mother—may her soul forever burn in the deepest bowels of Hell—had a proper funeral for Emmie's sake and nothing more. That was easy compared to having to fill out all the paperwork the social worker, Miss Hill, made Jesse handle. When he kept stumbling, Emmie took over and did the paperwork herself, giving it back for him to sign his name at the end.

Of course there was school to worry about, but I found an alternative for that. She could be homeschooled via internet while we were on tour. I bought her the best laptop and made the tech guy put all things she would possibly need on there, and a few things just for fun. I wanted to make sure that she didn't get bored while we were on the road.

Instead of packing up her clothes in that disgusting trailer, we took her shopping. She didn't want us to buy her anything, but she needed it. Deserved it. The only thing she ended up taking with her from her room was a backpack full of pictures. All of them were of us. Pictures of us when we were all younger. Things she might have gotten out of magazines or tabloids. She had started a scrapbook, something to help her when she missed us the most.

I was convinced we were smothering her by the last day before we were due to rejoin the tour in Oklahoma. We hadn't really let her out of our sight to do more than use the bathroom. I think we all had an irrational fear that someone was going to barge in and steal her away from us if we didn't have our eyes on her at all times. Emmie, however, didn't seem to mind it at all. She was just as glad to see us. For the first time since I had met her, she was smiling more often than not. There wasn't any fear in her big green eyes. With her mother gone, she had no one to fear.

Of course that didn't mean that people didn't have to fear her. As soon as we rejoined the tour, our manager, Rich Branson, ripped into us. As soon as greedy eyes landed on the newest addition to our group, his eyes narrowed on her. "You are nothing but trouble, you know that, princess?"

Green eyes burning with fire, Emmie said, "Don't call me princess, fucker."

"Nice. What a sweet little girl you are." Rich threw his arms in the air. "I can already see this is going to be fun."

"Back off, dude," Jesse told him. "Mess with Em, I'll fuck you up."

Rich walked away after that, muttering under his breath.

Chapter 4

From Baby Doll To…GODS, She's Beautiful!

It took us a while but we settled down. We got a new bus, one that didn't smell like Jack Daniels and sex so much. The guys and I had already agreed that there would be no sex on the bus. Emmie wasn't to be exposed to that at all. She had witnessed shit like that all her life with her mother. Our lifestyle wasn't going to be another whore house for her to have to deal with.

For the first few months we didn't let Emmie meet any of the other bands that were touring with us. The tour that we had been doing when her mother had died was already over and another one was just starting when Axton met Emmie again for the first time. To say I was on edge when Axton Cage hugged her close, like she was another one of his groupies, was an understatement.

"Little Emmie is growing up," Axton told her with one of his shitty grins that I knew got him laid on a daily basis. "Someone is going to be a hottie when she's legal."

My hands fisted at my sides. He didn't have to tell me that she was beautiful. Fuck, now that she had gained a little weight, she was even more stunning than when she first came to live with us. I hated how much I noticed the little things that made her so beautiful. So… female.

Thankfully Emmie took Axton's praises in her stride, putting him in the same category as the rest of us. Friend. She was just as comfortable with him as she was any of us. It was almost funny how she teased the rock god at times, and even I found myself laughing at it. Of course they were the times I could actually stand to be in the same room with Axton and Emmie.

By the time she was sixteen, none of us could deal with how gorgeous Emmie was. She was becoming sassier and that, on top of being beautiful, had guys coming out of the woodwork to just get her to notice them. Of course, she didn't. She was immune to any attention, good or bad. That didn't mean we didn't stress over it.

Jesse was the worst of the four of us. When he caught one of the sound guys talking to her, the guy's eyes eating up the sight of Emmie in her tight Demon's Wing tank top, skin tight jeans, and stiletto boots, Jesse had made sure the guy knew just how dangerous even thinking about Emmie like that would be to his health. A few loose teeth later and everyone that worked with us knew that she was hands—and eyes—off.

I was slowly going out of my mind. I was fighting my reaction to Emmie, which had only grown stronger and stronger with each passing month. I was a sick fucker. I hated myself in almost every way because I was feeling things that I had no business feeling for the girl that had once been my little baby doll.

It was a struggle to still be close to her, but the alternative was to give up the friendship—the connection that for me went soul deep. To do that would destroy me, so I learned to hide my sickness. To try and curb my needs, I found girl after girl and got lost in her, trying my best not to let Emmie sneak into my mind.

Seventeen came and slowly went by. I was sure that my desire would fade soon.

Right?

Wrong. So, so, so wrong!

--

"Happy birthday, Emmie!" Drake exclaimed.

"What is the one thing you want more than anything in the world?" Jesse asked.

We were all sitting in the back of the tour bus, which was parked in the parking lot of the arena we would be performing at tonight. But that was hours away, and we had dedicated the entire day to Emmie. Legal, eighteen Emmie.

She was cuddled between me and Shane, her head on my chest as Shane rubbed her feet that he had put in his lap. It was a bittersweet hell for me having her this close, smelling her shampoo and lotion that was subtle but no less seductive to my senses.

"I have everything I want right here," she told Jesse with a grin.

I tortured myself by running my fingers through the ends of her silky soft, auburn hair. "Don't be rotten, baby girl. What do you want to do?"

She shrugged, making her breast brush against my bicep. "I don't know. Can't we just veg out? Watch movies, eat junk food? I want pizza and Chinese food, and lots of ice cream and a cake. A huge cake."

"I'll have to run a marathon to get all of that off later," Shane laughed. "But if it's what you want, it's what you'll get."

"Okay, who's getting what?" Drake asked, already sucking on a bottle of Jack Daniels at barely ten thirty.

"I'll order the pizzas," I offered, picking up my cellphone from the table beside the couch I was sitting on.

"I'll go pick up the dessert and some movies. What are you in the mood for, sweetheart?" Jesse asked, getting to his feet.

"I want chocolate ice cream, and I don't care what the cake is. Just birthday cake. And toppings. I want lots of toppings for the ice cream. No nuts though." She kicked at Shane's legs when he tried to tickle her toes. "Jerk! Just for that I want to watch gore. Lots and lots of gore."

Shane groaned. "No. I'll throw up and then how am I going to play tonight?"

"Then be good to me!" She squealed when he grabbed for her feet again, already starting to tickle them. "No, no!" She kicked him hard in the side, making him release her. Of course she scooted back onto my lap, seeking the safety of my arms. "Don't let him, Nik!"

Good lord, the agony! Having that tight little ass brush against my groin was torture. Having her holding on and giggling so adorably only added to the pain. But it was a good pain. So fucking good!

With one arm I held onto her, keeping her against me. The other arm I warded Shane off, not wanting him to disrupt my lovely burden anytime soon. "Mine!" I claimed dibs on her teasingly while my heart screamed that it wasn't a joke. "Get your own."

"Right, so... chocolate, birthday cake, and the full collection of Full House it is." We all groaned and Jesse gave a wicked grin. "Unless the birthday girl has a better suggestion."

"Comedies. I want to laugh today."

By the time we were supposed to take the stage my stomach hurt. Half the pain was from being so full after all the junk we had gorged on all day. The other half was from laughing with Emmie and my band brothers so much. I was still grinning like an idiot when we closed the concert that night.

When I got back to the bus all I wanted to do was continue the way we had been all day long. Eat some cold pizza and stuff my face with another piece of the cake Jesse had produced that said: **Happy Birthday Emily**. The drummer had still been cursing about the bakery's mistake right before the show had started. Then I wanted to settle down and watch another movie with Emmie while the crew packed up and we headed out for the next city on our countrywide tour.

As soon as I stepped onto the bus I could hear Emmie giggling. The giggles were joined by a deeper chuckle, and my gut twisted with something close to jealousy. I didn't know why it bothered me that Jesse was already getting comfortable and doing the same things I had been planning on doing. Really, I hadn't even thought of my best friend in the whole scenario for tonight. With Drake and Shane off doing only Lord knew what, I had assumed he would be too.

I had wanted some alone time with Emmie. Alone time that may or may not have ended with her on my lap once more.

Pissed, I stomped through the bus like a kid that had been told he couldn't have a desired toy to play with. When I got to the back where our living room was, I found Jesse in the spot I had sat in most of the day… with Emmie snuggled up to him. Her head was on his chest, her arm wrapped across his waist. Her favorite blanket was tucked around her legs, and she was grinning in a way that made her soul shine through.

"I didn't think you would be back tonight," Emmie said without looking over at me from where I stood in the doorway.

I grimaced, a little sick to my stomach that she was so familiar with my normal routine after a concert. "There was something better waiting for me here," I told her honestly.

Her head turned then and she smiled up at me with that sassy tilt to her lips. "There's plenty of room on the couch for you."

I wasn't about to turn the invitation down. Sending Jesse a smug grin, which he rolled his eyes at, I sat on the other end of the couch. Once I was comfortable, I did something that I had wanted to do all day. I pulled her away from Jesse, tucked her into my side, and kissed her forehead. "Happy birthday, baby girl."

--

I woke with a warm weight on my chest. Something soft brushed across my cheek, and I blinked open my eyes to find Emmie sleeping soundly on top of me.

My body grew harder, because yeah, I had woken with my usual hard-on after dreaming of this beautiful girl. Her sweet smelling hair caressed my face, tickling me a little, and I just barely bit back a groan. With a soft sigh, she shifted, not disturbed by my slight movements. She had fallen asleep with one or the other of us over the last few years so this was nothing new to her.

For me, however, it was a mixture of Heaven and Hell. But I chose to enjoy this moment rather than let it make me miserable.

The last thing I remembered was Jesse turning in for the night around three o'clock. The bus was about to leave, and Drake and Shane had been in bed for more than an hour by then. With both of us getting tired but not ready to head off to bed just yet, I had turned on another movie and stretched out on the long couch. Emmie hadn't even asked before lying down beside me. As tiny as she was she didn't take up much room, and I had held onto her tight as the bus had pulled out into traffic and the opening credits started.

The movie hadn't been over before I had drifted off, still holding her close. She must have done the same, and then rolled on top of me in her sleep. Content for the moment, I ran my fingers over the soft skin of her bare arm, loving how silky it was. Goose flesh popped up as I continued the slow caresses.

Knowing that, at least in her sleep, she liked my touch thrilled me on a dark level, and I hated myself all over again. I couldn't do this. She trusted me, loved me as a friend and nothing more. She deserved better than what I could ever give her. I knew how hard it was to keep a meaningful relationship going when you were a rocker. I had watched the friends I had made over the years go through one horrible breakup after another.

Any stupid ideas that I might have harbored the day before were just that—stupid. Besides, I was sure that she didn't want the same thing. She hadn't so much as hinted that she even liked me as more than a friend.

Deflated, I moved so she was lying beside of me on the couch instead of on top of me. Emmie's big green eyes snapped open and she frowned up at me. "Are you okay?"

My lips lifted in a half smile. "Yeah, baby girl. I'm fine." I pulled her close, tucking her head under my chin. "Just fine."

Chapter 5

Sleep Aid?

Fighting something mentally is probably a million times harder than fighting a physical being. I've been in fights before. Some I've won, some I've lost. But once the fight was over, I walked away stronger, sometimes a little more proud, and that was that.

Fighting these feelings I had for Emmie?

Fuck that was hard. I couldn't just walk away from that. It didn't stop hurting, didn't stop eating at my mind and soul. I became a walking hard-on even after a night of anything-goes sex with some random groupie. It was getting to the point now that I didn't even see who I was having sex with. They all looked like Emmie, even when they were her complete opposite in appearance with big tits, curvy hips, and dark hair. When I was deep inside of them all I could think about was *her*.

Last night, as I took another girl against the bathroom stall in the bathroom backstage, I had even cried Emmie's name as I had come. The girl didn't seem to care, mostly because she was drunk and probably a little high. Still it had hit home that I couldn't keep going on like I was.

My desire wasn't the only thing growing stronger day by day. My feelings of possessiveness and jealousy were getting to the point that others were starting to notice. Not Emmie, of course. She wouldn't even think to question how I felt about her. She was blind to that. But Jesse and even Shane at times, had stopped and questioned me about how I was acting.

I wasn't in a good place. Our Australian tour had just kicked off, hot on the heels after the three months of being in Europe and six weeks in New Zealand. The stress of everything was piling up on me. Between being in a new city almost every other night, being unable to sleep without Emmie haunting my dreams, and trying to hide from my band brothers how fucked up I was, I was bone tired.

The only peace I had was when she fell asleep beside me. Thankfully she was doing that a lot lately. Emmie might not have realized that I was crazy about her, but she did see how exhausted I was. She was worried about me, and on top of taking care of everything else that we happened to need, she was making it her job to make sure I got enough sleep.

"I brought you some home remedy sleep aids," she told me as she dropped a bag at the end of my bed and flopped down beside of me.

I was stretched out on my bed, in yet another hotel, wearing nothing more than a pair of boxers. I was comfortable for what felt like the first time in months, happier than I had been in longer than I could remember. Why? Because Emmie was camping out in my room tonight. She had promised me all kinds of innocent things that to me were going to be sweet torture.

Pushing her hair back from her face, she opened the bag. "Tea. Milk which we can warm in the microwave. Massage oils that are supposed to help you fall asleep. What I paid for them, they had better induce a coma." She pulled her iPhone out of her hip pocket. "And some soothing music. I've been listening to ocean waves a lot lately. Want to give them a try?"

I shrugged. "Whatever you think is best, baby girl."

I watched contentedly as she made me a cup of some kind of herbal tea. It was bitter, even with sugar, but I didn't complain as I swallowed half the contents. My taste buds stopped working anyway when Emmie pulled her sleep pants off and tied her hair back with a black band.

"I don't want to get oil on my pants," she said as she turned on the ocean waves soundtrack and placed three different bottles of massage oils on the bedside table, not knowing that the sight of her in only a T-shirt and panties made my mind go blank of everything but the thoughts of doing things to her I had no right to think.

"Okay, roll onto your stomach," she commanded.

Oh, fuck! How was I supposed to lie on my stomach *and* let her touch me? Was it really possible to break your dick? Well, I guess I was about to find out!

Rolling over, I bunched my pillow up and hugged it while she climbed on top of me. When her panty clad pussy settled on my hips, I had to bite the pillow to keep from growling. She felt so warm even through two layers of clothing. All I wanted in the world in that instant was to roll her onto her back and discover if her hot little pussy smelled and tasted as good as it felt against my ass.

Emmie shifted to pick up the first bottle of massage oil. The scent of lavender and vanilla filled the air as she poured some of the oil into her hands. The scent set me at ease since those were the scents that I normally associated with Emmie. Even with my cock throbbing, drilling a hole into the mattress as it grew harder, my heart rate slowed a little. Breathing a sigh of contentment, I closed my eyes.

I could hear Emmie rubbing her hands together to warm the oil and then her soft hands touched my bare back. It was like being electrocuted, only in the best possible way. My blood started to heat, goose flesh popping up wherever she touched. Those wonderful hands of hers stroked firmly up my back and gently down over my spine.

A groan I was helpless to contain slipped free and Emmie giggled softly. "I'm glad you like this."

Each touch of her fingers and the flat of her palm were both soothing and distracting. My body was at war with itself, wanting to both relax yet ready to play. But I was greedy for her touch and didn't so much as move or speak as she worked those incredibly magical hands over my back for nearly an hour. The room began to fill with the scent of the oils, and I found that I was becoming addicted to the smell of lavender mixed with sweet vanilla.

"How are you feeling?" Emmie asked as she put the lid back on the last bottle of oil. "Feeling sleepy?"

I had to clear my throat before I could speak. "Something like that," I muttered. While she still had her back to me, I rolled out of bed and went into the bathroom. "Be right back," I called over my shoulder.

If there was any hope of getting any sleep tonight I had to take care of the pain in my dick. I closed the bathroom door and flipped the lock just to make sure that I had the privacy I needed. Leaning back against the door I pulled my throbbing cock from my boxers and squeezed the shaft.

It felt so good and I had to grit my teeth to keep from groaning in pleasure. My head fell back against the door, and I closed my eyes as I stroked myself. The fresh memory of Emmie's hands all over my back gave me all the visual I needed as I jacked off. I pretended it was her hands on my aching flesh, stroking me toward completion. My heart rate took off as my balls tightened, and I knew it was going to be over sooner than I had anticipated. Muttering a curse because I didn't want it to be over yet, I reached for a hand towel and wrapped it around the head of my dick as my release exploded from the tip.

When I could breathe evenly again I flushed the toilet and washed my hands, knowing that Emmie would bitch at me if I didn't. Opening the door, I found her already under the covers, her head on one of my pillows and a cup of warm milk ready for me on the bedside table. For a moment I just stood there in the doorway of the bathroom. With the lights dimmed it cast a soft glow over the bed and Emmie's skin. Her hair was spread over both pillows, and I pretended for a moment that we were a couple and I had every right to climb into bed beside her and make love to her until dawn.

"How are you feeling?" she asked with concern.

I moved away from the door. "I feel…" Like my heart is going to burst from my chest if I don't tell you how much I care about you. "…better."

"We can do this again tomorrow night if you want to," she offered, cuddling close when I crawled under the covers with her. "If you don't find something that will keep you busy after the show."

My gut twisted. She was so nonchalant about it, as if it wasn't a problem for her that I slept with random girls so often. Meanwhile I was left with a ball of guilt, as if I had cheated on her, after I fucked those girls. It was becoming more than I could handle, and I was getting to the point that I rarely sought out a girl to keep me company at the end of each show anymore.

I wrapped my arm around her and pulled her close, tucking her head under my chin. "Tomorrow night it is, baby girl."

Emmie's Enemy

"I hate her!"

"Why?"

"Because ..." Emmie broke off. "Just fucking because."

Jesse sighed. "I can't fix it if you don't tell me what's wrong."

"I don't need you to fucking fix it. Just let me be pissed, okay?"

I heard the raised voices coming from the bus before I even opened the door. When I heard how upset Emmie was I had a sudden urge to run for the hills. A pissed off Emmie was not something I wanted to deal with today. Three weeks into the Australian tour and I was ready for a break. Not just a few days, but a month long break from everything.

"I don't like it when you're pissed. Just tell me what happened," Jesse commanded.

Hearing my best friend consoling her made up my mind for me, and I opened the door to our tour bus. More and more I saw how close Jesse and Emmie were. Part of me knew that they were just friends, that Jesse would only ever think of her as his sister. He was a better man than I was, after all. But another part of me, the irrational part of me that was associated with Emmie and all my crazy feelings for her, didn't see it that way. That part saw every little thing my friend did as romantic, lover-like. I hated for them to be alone for even a moment. Hated to see him cuddling with her or see her laugh with him when I wasn't around.

Stepping onto the bus, their conversation became even clearer, and I stopped at the front to listen for another moment. I had no idea who *she* was that Emmie hated, but there weren't many *shes* to choose from. Other than Emmie, there was only about ten other females touring this go-round.

"I was just minding my own business, making sure that everything was ready for you guys tonight. I didn't even look in the bitch's direction. And she had the gall to come up to me and…" Emmie stopped and let out a high screech, venting some of her anger. "Never mind. It doesn't matter. I hate her, that's final."

"She's a little hard-core, I'll give you that, Em. But I hadn't gotten that vindictive bitch vibe from Gabriella before."

I frowned. Gabriella Moreitti? Emmie was having problems with the opening act's vocals? Why would they be arguing? It didn't make sense.

Unless… OtherWorld was also headlining our tour, and I had seen that Axton and Gabriella were sparking off of each other. Could the two girls be arguing because they both wanted Axton and were jealous of each other?

Not sure if I wanted to know the answer to that particular question, I moved to the back of the bus were Jesse and Emmie were still talking. "What's all the commotion about back here?" I demanded as I entered our living room.

Jesse shrugged. "Emmie and Gabriella got into it pretty heatedly backstage a while ago."

Emmie's eyes glared at me for a moment before she turned her head away, hiding her eyes from me. But not before I caught a glimpse of hurt and pain in those big green eyes. What had I done? I couldn't help but wonder because she had looked accusingly at me for that brief moment.

"Emmie doesn't get along with other members of her sex," I excused, frustrated with Emmie's sudden snub. "It's not exactly a surprise, Jess."

"I don't really give a fuck either way. But she started it with Emmie and now Emmie is upset. So something needs to happen here, bro."

I thrust my hands into the front pockets of my jeans. "Emmie is almost twenty years old now, Jesse. She can handle a little female squabble on her own."

I wasn't expecting the coffee cup to go flying by my head. I yelped and looked at Emmie. She was standing there with another coffee cup ready and waiting to be hurled at my head. She was almost shaking with her anger. "Fuck you, asshole!" And she threw the cup.

I had time to move out of the way this time. "What the hell is wrong with you?" I demanded, shocked by this sudden rage coming from her. "I didn't do a damned thing to you!"

"Just leave me alone, Nik. I'm done with it all anyway." She pushed past me and practically ran from the bus.

I turned to follow her because I was sure she had had tears in her eyes. I couldn't stand her tears. They were like acid to my soul. A big beefy hand caught my shoulder, stopping me from taking another step. "Don't. Just give her a little while to calm down."

My head drooped. "What just happened?"

Jesse sighed. "A bunch of idiots that refuse to open their eyes happened," he muttered.

Confused and not for the first time in as many minutes, I raised my head to ask him what he meant but he was already leaving me to follow after Emmie.

Chapter 6

Twenty-one

Planning a surprise party for the person that normally runs almost every aspect of your life is fucking hard.

Between trying to pay for the club, ordering the food, and making sure that only the right people were invited was no piece of cake. Yet somehow, between the four of us, we got it done. Of course I was reluctant to admit that Axton helped us out with a lot of it. Damned man, now he would get to share in the credit and Emmie was going to be all kinds of gushy over that.

Jesse offered to keep Emmie busy while we set up. I wanted to be the one to do it, but he spoke up quicker than I had and I didn't want to argue over it. It was just a little alone time with Emmie after all. I wasn't jealous, or even pouty about it. Not even a little bit…

Yeah, I'm a liar. I was completely jealous and more than a little pouty. I didn't speak to anyone as I filled balloons with helium and helped hang the banner that read: *Happy Birthday Emmie!* I wanted to be with Emmie, picking out the new tattoo with her that she said was the only thing she wanted for her birthday.

"Drake!" Shane called from the back of the club where he and Axton were setting up the gift table. "Put the fucking bottle down and help us out, brother."

I glanced over at my friend who was sitting at the bar watching us do the grunt work while he took a swig from an almost full bottle of Jack Daniels. I grimaced, wondering if Emmie would end up sleeping beside him tonight if the nightmares became unmanageable. I worried about Drake on a daily basis. Most days I prayed that he would hold on a little longer and be able to fight the demons that haunted him for just another day more.

"You got it covered, dude. There's nothing left to do."

He was right. The buffet table that groaned under the weight of all of Emmie's favorite foods was set up. The bartender was making sure that he had enough liquor to handle a shit load of rockers—plus Drake. The gift table was loaded with gifts of all shapes and sizes. I had hung red and black skull balloons throughout the club, because Emmie was a freak for skulls. And the banner which had taken me and Drake twenty minutes to put up was hanging perfectly.

Now all we had to do was wait for the birthday girl.

Taking a page out of Drake's book, I picked up a bottle and took a long pull from it. It was Patron, and I had learned that out of all the liquor in the world tequila fucked me up the worst. Tonight, I needed the numbness.

Six weeks ago I had realized that I wasn't just lusting after Emmie. I was full blown in love with that girl… woman. She was a woman now. One hundred percent. Either way, I loved her. And if she showed one little hint that she felt even a little of what I felt, then I would jump through the fires of Hell to make her mine.

But she hadn't. There was nothing to suggest that she even liked me as more than a friend, let alone wanted me. It was a hard pill to swallow, but I wasn't about to disrupt our friendship—the only fucking link I had to her—by telling her how I felt when she obviously didn't feel the same.

My head and heart were in agreement on that subject at least. My dick on the other hand? Not so much. I hadn't had sex in nearly two months now, a record for me. Two months of being unable to respond to the girls lining up to let me between their legs. Two months of only getting hard when Emmie was in the same room as me. My right hand was getting callused from all the jacking I was doing now.

I was down to half a bottle of Patron when the bouncer gave us the signal that Jesse and Emmie had arrived. The club wasn't overly crowded. All five of OtherWorld's band members had shown up. They adored Emmie, some more than others if the way Axton kept sniffing around was any indication. Rich had come. We had invited him out of respect for our manager, not because we had actually wanted him there. The two bands that we were on tour with at the moment were also in attendance, plus the road crew that had been with us for four years now. All in all there was a total of about thirty people, with only about twelve of them being female.

The bartender dimmed the lights and Shane lit the candles on the cake while we all gathered around the pink and black skull shaped birthday cake. We heard the door open and Drake and I started singing *Happy Birthday*.

"What?!" Emmie exclaimed when she saw what we had done. Her eyes grew bright and she had the biggest smile on her face as she came closer with Jesse right behind her. "Oh Gods!"

Everyone joined in on the birthday song, and she was openly laughing as she stood over the huge cake. I pushed Wroth aside so I could wrap my arms around her tiny waist and kissed her cheek after I had finished the song. "Happy birthday, baby girl. Make a wish." *Wish for me!* I silently begged.

Pulling her hair to one side, she bent over enough to blow out all twenty-one candles. When they had all winked out she turned and hugged me. "Thank you!" She kissed my cheek hard. "I love it."

My hands tightened around her waist for a moment too long before I let her go so she could hug everyone else. When she had finally hugged Jesse she went willingly into Axton's arms and let him kiss her on the cheek too. That was when I pulled my bottle of Patron back out and started chugging that shit.

"Okay, let's see this new tattoo," Shane commanded an hour or more later.

I raised my heavy head. "Yeah, let's see."

I regretted the words as soon as she started pulling her jeans down. All I could think was that Emmie was stripping in front of a room full of horny ass rockers. But my tongue stuck to the roof of my mouth and I couldn't voice my protests. Instead, I was helpless to do anything but sit there and watch as she exposed her hip.

It was bandaged but she carefully pulled the tape back and exposed a black heart with demon wings. My heart constricted when I saw four names in red ink in the middle of the heart. Drake. Jesse. Shane… Nik. I skimmed a shaky finger over my name.

How did I get over the fact that my name was now on her beautiful body?

--

If you want the truth, I didn't completely sober up after that night. I was half drunk for at least two weeks after that.

As soon as the numbness of the alcohol would start to fade I would start drinking again.

We went through four different cities during that time. Today we had arrived in city number five and a whole day ahead of schedule, due to a snow storm in Memphis that had been bad enough to shut the state of Tennessee down. Of course we had arrived to heavy rain showers in Tampa, and I was sure that it was going to start thundering soon.

Emmie's fear of thunder and lightning made me dream of her. I had lost count of the times she had climbed through my window when we lived next door to each other as kids because of her fear of thunder storms. Thunder always made me think of Emmie and her cuddled close to me as we would wait out the storms together. Of course I dreamed of her often anyway, but tonight the dream was particularly vivid.

I was stroking my dick when my tormenter appeared in the doorway of my hotel room. Fuck she was beautiful with the light from the bathroom highlighting her auburn hair and porcelain complexion. She was barefoot, which was just fine with me, but normally in my dreams Emmie came to me in thigh high boots and very little else.

I wiped a smear of my desire off the tip of my dick with my thumb and held out my hand to her. "I've been waiting all night for you. Come here, baby."

She didn't hesitate as she did as I asked. As soon as she was beside me I cupped her hand around my aching cock. The feel of her soft hands on my throbbing flesh was sublime. "Do you feel how much I need you?" I asked in a voice that didn't sound like my own it was so full of desire.

"Yes," was her husky answer that made me shiver with pleasure.

I loved that I had to teach her how to touch and stroke me. Emmie was innocent in my dream. So sweet and innocent. I had wanted to teach her all the amazing things about lovemaking for more years than I could actually admit to myself. I knew that she couldn't be that innocent in real life, though. She and Jesse had gotten even closer lately and then there was Axton.

Not wanting to think of either of those fuckers at the moment, I kissed my dream Emmie. She tasted of toothpaste, which might have thrown me off for a moment if I hadn't been drunk before I had fallen asleep. But under the taste of mint was her unique taste and it was so sweet. I was sure I hadn't tasted anything so sweet in my life and I told her so.

Graceful fingers combed through my hair and tangled in the thick locks. Her eagerness delighted me and I grinned down at her. "I'm not going anywhere," I promised.

"I need you, Nik," she cried.

I cupped her face, trying to take in every line of my dream Emmie. "I need you too, baby." She was so fucking beautiful it hurt to breathe for a moment. I kissed her, trailing down her jaw and neck, stopping only long enough to suck on her rapidly beating pulse at the base of her neck.

Stripping my dream Emmie was a treat in and of itself. I took my time, making sure that I licked every inch I exposed. When I got to the tattoo that had my name inside, I sucked and nibbled my way around the heart. "This is sexy as hell."

Only after I had my fill of her front did I turn her onto her stomach, the tattoo she had gotten shortly after she had turned eighteen spread across her back. The demon wings that Drake had designed specifically for her never failed to make me stop and stare. The words portraying her as ours—Property of Demon's Wings—said it all for me. Only I wished it said "Property of Nik" instead.

When my dick skimmed over her perfect ass, I grew twice as hard. I wanted in that sweet ass. Had dreamed of taking her there a dozen times over the years. When she eagerly spread for me, offering me whatever I wanted, I had to turn her down. I was harder than I could ever remember being in my life, and it was because it was her that I was making love to tonight. Even if it was just my dream Emmie, my body was getting what it wanted and my dick was nearly double in size in my need to have her.

To avoid temptation I turned her over and buried my face between her sweet smelling legs. If I had thought her kiss was the sweetest thing I had ever tasted, I had been severely wrong. How could a woman taste of such sweet nectar? I lapped it all up, smearing her liquid desire all over my face as I felt her come all over my tongue.

I wanted her to taste the sweet treat and kissed her without wiping her desire from my face. She stilled under me when she got that first taste, but then I felt her melting for me again and knew that she enjoyed the flavor of herself. Her teeth bit into my bottom lip, sucking her release from my mouth.

With an agonized groan, I rolled us so she was straddling my waist. This was what I liked… to have her on top while I watched those perfectly formed tits bouncing while she rode me hard. But I needed the words first, needed to hear what I was too much of a coward to ask for when I was awake.

"Tell me you are mine."

"I'm yours. All yours, Nik!"

I didn't think about a condom. The only sex I was having was with dream Emmie and I didn't need them so I stopped carrying them. So when she took all of me into her incredibly tight, agonizingly wet pussy I was bare. If I wasn't already asleep I was sure that I would have passed out from the sheer pleasure of feeling her stretching to fit me.

I hit a barrier and paused for only a moment before thrusting deep. My heart flipped at the realization that I was dream Emmie's first. Tears burned my eyes, but I blinked them away as she took me to the very hilt.

My fingers gripped her hips as she started to move. "Don't. Please don't move. I'm going to embarrass myself and blow in that sweet pussy way to soon if you move."

She leaned forward, kissing me while those tits that I loved so much skimmed over my chest. I cupped one with my left hand while the other held her firmly in place. Gods, she fit so perfectly in my hand. It was almost as if she was made for me, but I knew it was just my dream giving me an imagined form.

Her pussy grew slicker, wetter with need. When she whimpered my name I gave her what she needed. Her little clit was super sensitive as I rubbed it in tight little circles. She screamed my name as she rocked back and forth. She felt like pure heaven as her walls clenched around me with each glide up and down my shaft.

I knew she was close and I thanked all of those gods that she prayed to because I was holding on to my control by my fingernails. I increased the pressure on her clit and felt her body convulse at the same time her pussy flooded with her release. It was too much, too fucking much!

I came harder than I had in my entire life. Nothing could compare to how incredible making love to my dream Emmie was.

Dream Emmie was fading now that my body was spent. Darkness was rushing up to consume me and I was helpless to escape it.

The next morning I had a hell of a headache and I promised myself I wasn't ever going to drink like that again. Emmie was waiting for me downstairs in the hotel's restaurant, ready to have breakfast. I had to push down my urge to kiss her on the lips, knowing that I only had that privilege in my dreams.

While we waited for our meal to arrive I watched as she added more sugar than normal to her coffee. When she overdosed it with too much cream I realized that she wasn't even paying attention to what she was doing.

"Wake up, baby girl." I grinned when she muttered a curse and pushed her ruined coffee away.

"Sorry, I have a headache. I didn't sleep well last night."

My grin died. The storm the night before must have kept her up. "Sorry, Em. Did the storm get that bad?"

"Bad enough..."

Chapter 7

…Emmie…

Nik and the guys were on stage when I got the call I knew was coming.

My fingers trembled as I pressed the connect button on my phone and pressed it to my ear. I swallowed hard as I listened intently, my eyes were focused on the man singing one of my favorite songs to at least five thousand fans. Blinking back tears, ones that were more for the man I loved than myself, I told the person on the other end of the phone to start making the appropriate arrangements. Arrangements I had set up a year ago when Nik's mom had started going downhill in her fight with Alzheimer's.

While the guys finished up on stage, I got busy taking care of the other million and one things that would have to be done by morning. First I called Rich Branson and what a lovely conversation we had. Gods, I hated that fucker! While talking with him I surfed the net and found plane tickets for the five of us to get to California by dawn.

When the concert came to a close, I stood directly on the sideline of the stage and made sure that Shane didn't run off with the salivating groupie skanks that had been eye fucking him all night. Seeing my expression, he handed his guitar off to a stage tech and headed toward me along with his three band brothers.

Drake and Jesse reached me first, and I just squeezed their hands. They could guess what was wrong by the look in my eyes and they stepped behind me as I reached for

Nik. Those ice blue eyes turned stormy as I grasped his hands. I had to swallow twice before I could get the words out. "I'm so sorry. She's gone, Nik."

The agony on his face at my words nearly crippled me, but I had to be the strong one here. Nik needed me and I'd let him lean on me for as long as he had to. Those eyes that haunted my dreams as well as my waking hours filled with tears, and he pulled me against him. No sound left him. He just held on to me and didn't let go.

My arms held him close, rubbing my hands up and down his tense back. His pain soaked into me, making it hard to breathe for a moment. Jesse squeezed his shoulder as Drake and Shane surrounded us. "I'm sorry, bro."

Nik sucked in a deep breath, his hold on me easing as he took half a step back. "What do I need to do?" he whispered brokenly.

"Nothing," I assured him. "I made sure that everything was set up when she had the feeding tube put in. I told the administrator to follow the plan we talked about …" He really didn't need to know all of that. We had argued about it for several weeks before he had finally let me make the funeral arrangements for the future event of his mother's death. I had hated myself, but I knew that he wouldn't have been able to make the decisions that needed to be made when the time did come and Sarah passed on.

"I have to tell Rich that we are leaving the tour."

I gave him a tiny smile. "No, Nik. I've already taken care of all of that. Everything has been arranged from the flight to the car that is going to be waiting on us when we land. I even called Tommy and told him we were going to use his house while we are in town."

I had hated talking to that old pervert nearly as much as I had hated talking to Rich. Tommy Kirkman wasn't exactly my brand of rocker with his taste for overly young girls, but my guys respected him and looked up to the old rocker who had taken them under his wing and shown them the ropes. So I tried to keep the peace.

I was lucky to get a flight that had room for all five of us. Of course we were spread out. Drake and Shane were all the way in the back by the bathrooms and Jesse somewhere in a middle aisle with a few business men. The only two seats beside of each other that I had been able to get were close to the front of the plane and Nik asked me to sit with him.

I tried to stay with him as much as I could in between going to the bathroom because of the air sickness I always got. There had been no time to get a prescription for the patches that normally eased my discomfort, so I struggled through. Being close to Nik, knowing that I was helping even a little bit, soothed something inside of me. I tried to rub his back, but he just wanted to hold my hand.

It was only a three hour flight, but we were all exhausted by the time the plane touched down at LAX. Aunt Sarah, as we had all called her, except for Nik who called her Mom, was the only decent female I have ever came into contact with. Drake and Shane's mother had been nice, but she had worked all the time and I had rarely seen her the few years I knew her.

While Aunt Sarah had been kind, she had still been distant with me. I didn't hold it against her. I knew that she thought I would one day turn out like my mother, and that she hadn't wanted her son to get pulled into that type of lifestyle. I had made myself a promise at the age of five that I was never going to let myself become my mother. If I was ever lucky enough to have a child I would devote my life to being the best mom. My kids would never have to wonder if they were going to get fed that day, or sleep with one eye open just so they wouldn't be taken by surprise by a midnight beating.

The limo was waiting and we all climbed in for the trip to Tommy Kirkman's house in Beverly Hills. Tom was out of the country for the next year or so, business or pleasure I still wasn't sure. He tended to mix the two anyway. It made relaxing in the man's house that much easier. I hadn't told the guys but when I was seventeen Tom had tried to seduce me. One try and that was all he needed to know not to fuck with me again.

There were still several hours to go before we had to go to the nursing home to make sure that everything was in order. I hoped that Nik wouldn't want to go, that Jesse or Shane could just go with me to sign the papers that needed my attention. But when I suggested Jesse go, Nik went a little crazy and stormed off toward the room he normally claimed as his when we stayed with Kirkman.

Jesse's big hand touched my shoulder gently and I covered it with my own, comforted just having my friend so close. I wasn't sure what it was about Jesse, maybe the fact that he was the one that had always played the role as my mother and father, but I always needed him close or I began to feel anxious. I had an odd connection to all of my guys. Shane was like my best friend while Drake was just like a brother to me.

And then there was Nik. I needed him in my life just as much as I needed the other three, but with Nik I was always being pulled in two different directions. He was my friend. He was the man I loved. I couldn't have it both ways and had learned early on that he only thought of me as his little sister. The girl he had spent the majority of his life taking care of.

I was okay with that. Really, I was. And for the most part I could handle the skank groupies that warmed his bed on a nightly basis.

Oh, who was I kidding? It was driving me crazy.

Leaving Jesse and the others in the living room, I followed after Nik. His door was unlocked and I barely knocked before opening it and glancing inside. My heart broke for him when I saw that he was sitting on the edge of the bed with his head in his hands. I shut the door softly behind me and went to him.

Dropping to my knees in front of him, I touched his hands gently. I had such wonderful memories of those hands on me from just a few weeks ago, but I put those thoughts out of my head as I wrapped my arms around him. He buried his face in my neck and I felt his tears falling onto my skin. His hands caressed down my back and then I felt his hot, rough hands touching my bare skin under my T-shirt. Being skin to skin with Nik was like being offered a glimpse into paradise. It was enough for me because I knew it was all I would ever have from him.

How long I sat there on my knees just holding onto him, I wasn't sure. My legs had long since fallen asleep when Nik raised his head. "Will you stay with me until we have to go?"

"I'll stay as long as you need me, Nik," I promised.

I thought I saw a flash of something intense cross his face but was too tired to question it as I stood. For the next few hours I lay in bed with him. One arm was under his head while the other wrapped tightly around my shoulders.

His fingers played with the ends of my hair like they always did, and I wondered if the action was just as soothing for him as it was for me. Neither of us spoke and I let myself relax to the sound of his steady heartbeat under my ear as I rested my head on his lean, muscled, hard chest.

The sun came up but we stayed where we were. It was after eight before he finally moved around, trying to work some of the kinks out of his stiff body. When he left me to shower, I took a moment to make a few necessary phone calls before going to shower in my own room.

Over the next two days I stuck to Nik's side like glue. It was where I wanted to be the most, and I was so thankful that it was where Nik wanted me too. It was like a dagger shredding my heart as I watched him silently cry while his mother was slowly lowered into the ground.

Aunt Sarah was the last of the family we had, except for Drake and Shane's dad and sister back in Ohio that they didn't acknowledge. So now it was officially just the five of us. We only had each other, and that was okay with me. Those four guys were all I had ever had anyway.

We returned to the tour and everything began to get back to normal.

Until I started getting sick.

Chapter 8

What's Wrong With Em?

    I didn't think I was going to get over my mom's death. Even with my band brothers and Emmie to help me through it all, I was still having a difficult time over two months later. She had been special, a one of a kind loving person, and I felt cheated that she was gone.

    Being so out of it I didn't notice how sick Emmie was until I heard her throwing up on the tour bus one morning. At first I thought it was Drake because he was always in there first thing in the morning emptying his system of the poison he had filled it with the night before. So it came as a shock when I saw Emmie coming out of the bathroom a few minutes after I heard the toilet flush.

    I didn't say anything right away. After all, I wasn't sure if it was something serious or not. When I mentioned it to Jesse later that morning he looked disturbed. We talked and I started putting a few things together. Emmie was sleeping all the time and she had lost weight, not to mention the mood swings that I hadn't questioned until now. When I looked at her a few hours later I saw that she was skin and bones, and she hadn't had any weight to lose to begin with.

    Jesse and I cornered her that afternoon as the bus drove toward another city for yet another concert. We were all burnt out, and I suspected that the heavy pace was taking it's toll on Emmie just as much as it was the rest of us. Maybe more. We didn't really think about what she had to do to keep our lives simple. She was always taking care of something, planning ahead so that everything ran smoothly for us. We were taking the summer off, having our first vacation since we had hit it big. Just a few more days, two more concerts in Galveston, and we were headed to Florida for three full months.

Emmie being Emmie, she pointedly refused to go see a doctor at first. When Jesse told her just how worried we were, she reluctantly gave in. It shouldn't have bothered me when she agreed for him, but it did. And when she crawled onto his lap to comfort him because he was so worried, I saw red for a minute.

I had to sit there and watch them. Emmie was wrapped around Jesse like she belonged in his arms. It felt like a punch directly to the chest, but after a few minutes of hating my best friend I realized that no matter how I felt all I really wanted was for Em to be happy. If Jesse was what she wanted, I would step aside and let her have him.

I prayed that wasn't the case though. It was getting harder and harder to hide how I was feeling. A song had been scrambling around my brain for a few weeks now and I knew that I had to get it out. Maybe, just maybe, once I had the song ready and Emmie heard it she would realize that I loved her…

Perhaps she would be able to come to love me too.

When Emmie fell asleep in Jesse's lap, I had to get up. I couldn't watch them sleeping together. Walking through the moving tour bus, I went straight through the sleeping quarters without stopping. Shane and Drake were already asleep, taking up one set of the bunks. I could have climbed onto the top bunk on the other side, which was my usual bed anyway, but I wanted to feel closer to Emmie.

She always took the front of the bus. It was her own space and we usually respected it as hers. Her computer was on the long table in front of the couch that she normally slept on, and there were a dozen different papers scattered around the computer. I stretched out on the couch on my stomach, hugging her pillow under my head. Breathing deep, I took in the scent of her shampoo— lavender and vanilla.

It gave me a little peace from the ache seeing her with Jesse caused, as well as the nagging worry I felt after opening my eyes to just how sick she was now. A few lines from the song I was working on clouded my brain, and I hummed the lyrics a few times as I slowly drifted to sleep.

Gentle yet firm hands pushed on my shoulder. I turned over, still half asleep until I felt Emmie snuggle against my bare chest. She put her head on my chest and closed her eyes. My heart swelled as I wrapped her safely in my arms. Tenderly, I brushed a kiss over her forehead, breathing in her sweet scent.

"You don't know how happy you just made me," I whispered, knowing that she was already asleep and couldn't hear me.

--

As soon as the song was finished I knew I had to sing it. Emmie had to know what I was feeling and I needed her to know before we started our vacation. I didn't want to spend the entire summer hiding how much I needed her.

Tonight was our last concert and I was nervous. Not even during our very first concert had I felt so nervous. I went through the song with Drake several times backstage, and he was giving me some pretty evil looks when he realized just what the new song was about. I ignored him.

The Rocker That Holds Her

When we took the stage, I promised the audience a new song later in the night just so I wouldn't chicken out and not perform it after all. Greedy for new material from us, I knew our fans wouldn't let me forget.

With the lights flashing and bouncing to the beat of Jesse's drumming, I was a little blind to what was happening on the sidelines of the stage. I knew Emmie was standing just out of sight and from time to time I would get a glance of her as she paced while she handled business with her phone. The concert was only a few songs from being over, and I was determined that the next song was going to be for Emmie.

Still singing *Ashes*, I glanced toward where I had last seen her.

I nearly stumbled over the words when I saw her kissing Axton. My heart felt like it was going to explode, my eyes clouded with rage, and it was only because I knew the song so well that I was able to finish the fucking thing. Terrified that I was too late, that Axton was the one she wanted, I rushed to get the next song set up.

Unable to bring myself to look in Emmie and Axton's direction again. I couldn't help but wonder what Axton was even doing in Galveston. I knew that he should have been in California with Gabriella Moreitti since they were supposed to be an item now. It pissed me off that he had dropped in right when I was about to make my move.

Drake sat on a stool beside of me with his acoustic guitar and the lights dimmed around us. I took a deep breath, determined that I wasn't about to let my fucking friend ruin what I hoped to achieve.

You forced my lonely and cold heart to beat

The Rocker That Holds Her

No longer waiting in the shadows resigned to the same defeat.
Now there is an Ember that has sparked a flame,
Bringing me back to life with just a smile.

I was sure that Jesse and Shane were lost, knowing that I wrote only from my soul and life experience. With each line I sang I felt tenser and had to fight with myself not to look toward Emmie. Somehow I got through the song, my chest shaking from how hard my heart was beating.

Finally it was all over. As soon as Drake played the last cord I was off the stool and rushing backstage, ready to face Emmie's reaction to the song.

She was gone. There was no sign of her or Axton, and my heart dropped to the ground. But as I stood there, glancing around for the girl that I was stupidly in love with, the disappointment turned to anger. I wasn't sure who I was angrier with. Emmie for not noticing before how much I loved her, or myself for not telling her sooner.

Now she was off with Axton, doing only gods knew what, and I was left feeling empty.

Muttering a curse, I stomped off. I didn't care where I went, just as long as I got away from everyone. I hated the world, the universe. I thought of hooking up with some random girl, taking her back to the hotel and making sure that Emmie knew that I wasn't going to keep wasting my time waiting for her to open those beautiful green eyes.

By the time I got to the hotel my phone had started ringing. Seeing it was Axton, I decided to turn it off. I didn't need him rubbing it in my face that he had gotten what I wanted. That shithead knew exactly how I felt about Emmie and hadn't thought twice to use it against me.

Like always, there was the usual line of groupies hanging out by the rear of the hotel. They were the hopefuls that hadn't gotten to see the concert but were still determined to warm one of our beds for the night. The idea to hook up was squashed, however, even as I started to take my pick.

I couldn't do it. The thought of touching someone that wasn't Emmie made my stomach cramp and I turned away. Up in my room I ordered a bottle of whiskey and some food. The whiskey kept my attention diverted for a good hour, and I was feeling more than a little mellow when I decided to turn on my phone.

If Emmie was off with Axton having fun then I was going to ruin it. The phone took it's time rebooting and I was about to bring up Emmie's name when the amount of missed calls from Axton popped up on the screen. I knew that Axton wouldn't have been calling that much unless it was seriously important. The guy had better things to do, more stupid ass pranks to play.

My stomach was in knots as I listened to the first message:

"Where the fuck are you? I have Emmie at the emergency room. She's seriously sick, man. Come here as soon as you get this!"

My feet were moving even as the next message started playing automatically. "What is the matter with you fuckheads? Emmie is sick and you idiots are off getting laid! Some family you are."

"They won't tell me what's wrong because I'm not family. Get here. NOW!" The third message ended and the fourth started. "Alright, Armstrong. I see how it is. You don't really care at all, huh? All those drunken confessions of loving Em were just bullshit. Well, I'm not so stupid. If you won't step up and take care of her, I fucking will. She likes me, you know."

I nearly crushed my phone as I hit the end button, deleting all of the other messages without listening. Instead of letting his words get the better of me, I tried to stay focused. I had to find the guys, get to the hospital, and make sure that Emmie was okay.

By the time I found the others and we got to the hospital, more than two hours had passed since the first phone call. Axton was standing by the entrance, his phone still to his ear as he tried to call Jesse's number again. The relief that was on his face when we stepped out of the taxi was evident. It only made my fear and anxiety level rise.

"About fucking time, dickwads!" he exploded and punched me in the arm.

"How is she?" Jesse demanded before I could ask.

Axton shook his head. "She was unconscious when we got here, but she's stable now. They gave her fluids and the doctor was talking to her the last time I peeked in."

"Thanks for helping her. You can go now," I told him, not caring that I was acting like a bastard. I should have been shaking my friend's hand, thanking him on my knees for taking Emmie to the hospital when she had needed help.

"So you can take over? Looks like you haven't been doing such a good job so far." The rock god's eyes darkened, looking almost menacing. "I think I'll stay. Maybe finish what we started earlier tonight when she let me kiss her."

I could picture my fist connecting with his jaw, imagined the bone breaking. As I started to take a step toward the prick to do just that, Jesse grabbed my arm and pulled me toward the door. "Thanks, Ax!"

Shane was already asking a nurse which room Emmie was in. "Are you a family member?"

Drake nodded his head, answering for his brother. "Yes, ma'am. Em is our sister." The lie was something that slipped off the tip of their tongues easily. From the time Emmie had come to live with us that was what we told most people. For me, it had been a harder pill to swallow when saying those words.

The nurse didn't question either Shane or Drake. She just glanced down at her iPad and then gave them her room number. I kept a few paces back from my friends as we rushed toward her room. I was still seething after the encounter with Axton.

A doctor was sitting beside Emmie's bed when we entered her room. She was deathly pale and all thoughts of destroying Axton or being angry at Emmie evaporated. Gods, she looked so small lying in the hospital bed. She was covered with a blanket to her waist, and an IV with rapidly dripping fluids was attached to one of her arms. I could see the wires from what I could only guess was a heart monitor, and I felt like I was going to vomit.

So close. So fucking close! I ... We had nearly lost her.

Oh, dammit all to hell. *I* had nearly lost her. There I had admitted it to myself.

The guys were apologizing to Emmie. We should have gotten here sooner. We should have been the ones that had taken her to the hospital in the first place. Axton was right. We hadn't been taking good enough care of Emmie.

I turned my full attention on the doctor, determined to find out exactly what was going on with Emmie and how to make her better. My fear was that it was some kind of cancer, but we had the money to take care of her. I had seen the effects of it with Liam Bryant's sister, Marissa, and knew that as sick as Emmie had been it could very well be the same thing.

The first question was going to be the hardest, but I manned up and asked. "What's wrong with her?" The second question was just as important and I needed to know it more than the first, if for no other reason than to save my sanity. "Is she going to be alright?"

The doctor, a man that looked barely older than me or the others, glanced down at Emmie for a brief moment before clearing his throat. It wasn't lost on me that he appeared to be intimidated by the four of us. I knew that we could look like scary fuckers. Truth was the doctor had every reason to be intimidated. With the exception of Emmie, we didn't give a fuck about anything or anyone. We were bastards. And if this doctor thought about standing in our way, none of us would think twice about fucking him up.

"She came in severely dehydrated," the doctor informed us and went on to explain that he was keeping her overnight for observations, but he had no idea what was wrong with Emmie.

Jesse went off, demanded the idiot doctor get off his ass and do some tests. When Emmie linked her fingers with his and calmed him down almost immediately, jealousy reared its head for the second time that night, and I had to look away.

The doctor suggested that we leave and I was glad that Shane was the one to speak up because I knew I would have taken the doctor's head off if I had to do it. There was no fucking way we were leaving her now! The doctor was talking under his breath to himself when he left.

Emmie was sandwiched between two huge men as Drake and Jesse hugged her tight. I don't know why I wasn't jealous of Drake, or even Shane. Maybe it was because Drake had risked so much—and lost even more—to protect Emmie when we were younger. I knew he and his brother would never, ever touch Emmie.

Jesse on the other hand? Jealousy ate me up. It made me hate the man that had been my best friend for nearly my whole life. Hating Jesse left me feeling almost as empty as loving Emmie did.

"You should have seen a doctor before now," Jesse scolded.

"It was nothing. I'm fine now." Emmie tried to making it sound like she hadn't almost died tonight.

Hearing her make light out of something that could have ended differently in a horrible way if Axton hadn't been around was the last straw. All of my emotions, everything from the nervousness of singing that stupid song, to the jealousy and hurt at seeing her with Axton started to boil over.

I couldn't hold it all in a second longer. "It isn't nothing!" I kicked the little round rolling chair across the room, not caring that it bounced against the opposite wall. I found myself raking my fingers through my hair and pulling on the ends. "Axton said you were unconscious when he got you here. Unconscious Emmie! Don't you understand how fucking serious this is? Has it slipped your attention that people die from dehydration?"

When she just stared up at me with her big green eyes wide with surprise I lost it on a whole new level. She looked so small in that fucking bed, so sick and still so goddamned beautiful. I turned away from her and my band brothers and took all my pain and frustration out on the wall as I punched it.

The wall was cement or some other stone. It broke the skin on my knuckles and the ache that shot through my hand and up my arm did nothing to pull my mind from the turmoil it was in now. Leaning on the wall that I had just tried to destroy, I let my tears fall.

Behind me the room was in almost complete silence, except for the constant pacing of Shane and my deep breathing.

"Nik …" Emmie's voice was soft, gently commanding me to face her. I could no more deny her than stop breathing. Scrubbing my throbbing hand over my damp face, I turned around. Jesse and Drake were still on either side of her, but she held her arms out to me. My heart jumped. She wanted me to hold her?

My feet took me over to her before I could even comprehend that I was walking. Drake moved aside and I dropped carefully down on the edge of her hospital bed. Her arms and hands were cold as they wrapped around me and she pulled my head to her chest. "I'm okay," she whispered in my ear, and I couldn't keep from shuddering. I needed her reassurance and soothing touch. "I'm here."

A sob escaped me before I could call it back, and I held onto her tight. "I'm sorry, Emmie," I told her, silently begging her to forgive me. "I'm so sorry."

Chapter 9

What. The. FUCK!

Sleeping in a chair beside of Emmie's bed in her private room wasn't the worst place I had ever fallen asleep. Still, it wasn't anywhere close to being comfortable, and I woke with a stiff neck and a desperate need for coffee.

The night before flashed through my mind like a bad dream, and I opened my eyes to find Emmie holding Jesse's hand. I refused to let my jealousy get the better of me today, so I offered to get coffee. Standing, I let myself have the small comfort of kissing her on the forehead and asked if she needed anything. When she asked for a lemon-lime soft drink, I promised her I would find her one and gave in to my need for just one more touch of my lips to the soft skin on her forehead.

The nurse that had practically been salivating at the sight of Shane the night before showed me where the vending machines were before her shift ended. Somehow I carried the four cups of coffee and the soft drink back down to Emmie's room without burning myself. Drake and Shane were up and moving around by the time I got back.

Despite the four bags of fluids that had been pushed into Emmie through the IV in her arm, she was beyond thirsty. No sooner had I handed over her drink she had gulped it down. After years of spending time with nasty rockers she was a pro at belching and didn't bother to keep one in after swallowing half her drink.

We were still laughing and teasing her when a nurse with short hair walked in. She took charge for about five minutes. Emmie's vitals were taken and Shane made a run for it before the nurse started on Emmie's IV. After explaining the doctor's orders to Emmie, the nurse handed her a prescription for vitamins.

Really? Vitamins? As sick as Em had been, all she needed was vitamins? That really didn't make sense to me. Apparently I wasn't the only one confused because Jesse and Drake started to question the woman.

"Guys …" Emmie tried to intervene and I wasn't completely blind to the nervous look on her face.

When the nurse laughed I got a bad feeling. "A baby doesn't qualify as a serious illness, honey."

I was sure my head had actually exploded. The word *baby* kept bouncing around in my head until I was sure I was going to lose my mind. No. I had misheard. That had to be the answer. A misunderstanding. I was still half asleep and exhausted from work and the emotional night before.

"What?" I heard Jesse's strangled question.

"… the …" Drake was saying something but I couldn't really focus on it.

Running my fingers through my hair, I didn't even try to stop the curse from exploding from my mouth. "FUCK!"

Jesse looked wild as he charged over to Emmie's bed. "What the fuck is she talking about? A baby?"

Emmie's nervousness seemed to intensify and she seemed to struggle for a moment before she sighed. "I'm pregnant."

The nurse excused herself. She could no doubt see that a war was about to break out in the room and wanted to be out of the line of fire. Smart woman. Because I was a fucking bomb about to explode.

"How is that possible?" Drake demanded and Emmie actually laughed.

"You mean you don't know the how, Drake?"

"Don't try to be cute, Em. You know exactly what the fuck I mean."

When Shane entered the room and the others filled him in on the reasons for our yelling. I was shaking. Emmie was pregnant. Someone had touched her. Oh fuck. I had been okay when I had only assumed that she was involved with someone. Now that I knew it was a reality, I couldn't handle it. The woman I loved wanted someone else.

"Who?" I wasn't sure if I had whispered the question or screamed it at her.

"What?" Emmie looked confused by my question.

I had kind of gone numb when the nurse had announced that Emmie was pregnant. Now it was wearing off and I was cracking from the inside out. "Who, Emmie? Who is the father?" I couldn't stop looking at Jesse, or the rage that slowly started to consume me as I realized that he had actually touched her. "Or do I already know?"

"What?" She sounded shocked.

"What the fuck, Nik!" Jesse yelled at me. "You think I would… have you lost your fucking mind, bro? She might be hot, but I would never touch her! She's like my sister."

"I don't believe you." I had seen with my own eyes how close they were. That closeness had only intensified over the last few months. "I see the way you look at her. I see how she is always clinging to you." And it killed me a little more every time I saw it.

"Nik..." Emmie's voice was soft, trying to soothe me. My eyes went to her. In that moment I wanted to feel absolutely nothing for her, but I couldn't turn off my feelings. A small part of me hated her. "Nik, Jesse isn't the father."

The relief I felt at her words was short lived. Not Jesse, not the man that had had my back since we were little kids. But if not Jesse, then who. "Who, Em?" I was in front of her in a matter of seconds. Leaning down with my hands on either side of her body, I forced her to keep eye contact with me. I needed the truth. "Who the fuck touched you?" I yelled at her.

For a moment I saw fear in her eyes. She had no clue why I was so mad, and that only increased my anger. I wanted to scream at her to open her fucking eyes. She was so blind to how much I cared!

Before I could open my mouth to do just that, Drake pulled me away. "Stop it. Can't you see that she is terrified of you right now?"

"Just tell me who!" I demanded.

"Why?" There were tears in her voice. "Why do you have to know so badly?"

"So I can kill him." I screamed, fighting my own tears.

A tear fell from her eyes. "What is wrong with you, Nik? Why are you acting like this?"

"Axton?" I made a guess, knowing that the fucking douche bag had to be the only other possibility. "He was sniffing around a few months ago. Was it him? I saw him with his hands on you last night." I tried to get free of Drake's hold. I wasn't sure what I was going to do if I got loose. Shake the truth from her? She wasn't going to willingly tell me. "Was it him?"

"No!" she cried.

"Who?!"

Jesse put himself between me and Emmie, his back turned away from me as he urged Emmie to tell me. "Tell him, Em."

"Someone in this room?" If it was Shane, and I hadn't even suspected he was after her, I would…

"Yes," she whispered.

I struggled harder, ready to rip into Shane. No fucking way. I could almost tolerate Jesse touching Em, but Shane? No. No. NO!

I needed her to confirm it. I needed her to say who the father was. "Who, Em? Just tell me who." I was close to tears now, my voice giving me away as it dared to crack.

"Nik …"

"WHO?!" I bellowed.

"YOU!"

--

I was too stunned to move. In fact, I was sure that I lost all major mobility for a few minutes. One minute Drake was holding onto me, making sure that I didn't hurt anyone. I knew that I wouldn't have hurt Emmie. No matter how enraged I had been, I never would have touched her with violence. Jesse, on the other hand, would have been another story.

A mixture of disbelief and euphoria battled inside of me. No way had Emmie just said that the baby was mine. Right?

Right?!

She had just said the words. I had heard them. I wasn't still asleep in that damned chair beside of her bed and was dreaming this whole thing. All around me the room was quiet, except for the heart wrenching sobs coming from the woman I loved.

Looking up at her from the floor where I had fallen to my knees I whispered, "What?"

"You, Nik." Her voice broke on yet another sob. "You are the father."

I shook my head, still not quite believing that she had just given me something I had only dreamed of. "No. I … No …"

Trembling fingers wiped away rapidly falling tears. "Yes, Nik."

"It was a dream. I dreamed that night." I got to my feet as quickly as my shaking legs would allow and pushed Jesse out of my way before falling to my knees beside her bed. "Right?"

Emmie's eyes looked down at the blanket still covering her waist and shook her head. "I'm sorry, Nik. I'm sorry I took advantage of you. Please…" her voice broke again and my heart clenched painfully "…please don't hate me."

What the fuck was she talking about now? I was pretty sure I knew what night we had made the baby growing inside of Emmie. The next morning I had woken with the scent of sex in the air but had thought that I had just gotten myself off in the middle of the night. It wouldn't have been the first time that I had jerked off while I dreamed of Emmie.

Fuck! A million questions filled my mind. Had I hurt her that night? Had I been gentle like she had needed and deserved? Did she enjoy it? I suddenly feared that I had ruined sex for her.

The snickering of my band brothers pulled me back from my wondering. Emmie glared at them over my head. "This is not funny. I practically raped him!"

I couldn't help it. It would have taken a man with a lot more willpower than I would ever claim to have to not have started laughing. But when I saw the look on Emmie's face—anger, fear, and maybe even a little humiliation—the laughter stopped dead, and I shook my head at her.

"Come on, Em. There is no way that you could have taken advantage of me. It's not rape when it's consensual, baby," I assured her.

The tears started falling all over again. "You didn't know it was me, Nik. You thought I was one of the groupies."

"The fuck you say!" I exploded. How could she even think that? "I might have been drunk, but I knew it was you the entire time, Emmie. I've been dreaming about it for a lot longer than I should have. That's why when I woke the next morning I thought nothing of it."

Behind me the guys made sounds of anger mixed with disgust. "Too much info, dude. Too much info. We don't need to know that shit."

I ignored Jess as I continued to watch Emmie. She looked stunned, maybe as stunned as I had been to find out I was her baby's father. Her eyes widened and I thought I saw something close to elation cross her beautiful face.

Could I have been wrong all this time? Had Emmie been fighting her own feelings for me while I had been doing the same with my feelings for her? I wanted to ask her about it then and there, along with about a million other questions.

"Emmie ..."

The suddenness of the hospital door opening stopped me from asking her anything. We were ordered out so the nurse could help Emmie dress. When I tried to protest, to tell the old hag to fuck off because I had more important things to sort out, Emmie took hold of my hand. My entire body felt as if I had been electrocuted by that simple touch.

"It's okay, Nik. I'll be out in a few minutes."

Jesse helped me to stand. "Let's go, bro. There is plenty of time to talk later. She isn't going anywhere."

That was the only thing I was sure of at the moment. Emmie wasn't going anywhere I wasn't. We had plenty of time to sort out our life, our future together.

The door closed behind Jesse just as I leaned back against the opposite wall with Drake. Thankfully Shane had gone ahead to grab us a cab. I didn't think I could have handled his pacing right then.

Jesse bumped my shoulder as he stepped back beside of me. I grimaced because now I had something else to deal with. The rage in my friend's ever changing dark eyes told me that I had a beating coming before his words confirmed it.

"It's coming, Nik."

I nodded my head, knowing that I deserved anything that Jesse, Drake, and Shane threw at me. I had done the one thing that we had spent the last six years making sure no other guy could attempt to. I had not only taken Emmie's virginity while wasted, I had gotten her pregnant too. As happy as I was about both, I was deeply ashamed of myself too.

She deserved better than this.

Minutes later the hospital door opened and the nurse pushed Emmie out in a wheelchair. Of course she had her phone at the ready, no doubt getting ready to work on something for the band. Jesse snatched the phone from her at the same time I saw the shiny piece of paper in Emmie's other hand.

"What's that?" I asked, nodding to what looked like a grainy black and white picture.

She handed it over before the nurse started pushing her toward the elevator. "It's an ultrasound picture of the baby... It's a girl."

I couldn't keep my fingers from trembling as I took the picture from her. It took me a moment to understand what I was looking at. It wasn't until we were nearly on the ground floor when I figured out what was what on the picture. The outline of a hand, the shape of a foot. The baby came into focus and I couldn't help smiling even as I felt my throat choked with emotion.

This was our baby. My baby ...

Emmie was the mother of my child!

Chapter 10

Stop Being A Fucking Coward

The flight from Texas to Florida was nowhere near fun. The guys and I sat and stressed over how sick Emmie seemed to be. She had always suffered from air sickness, but all the vomiting on top of just getting out of the hospital for dehydration had us on a razor's edge of anxiety. Less than half an hour before we were due to reach our destination, I was ready to demand the captain to land at the nearest airport so we could take Emmie to see a doctor.

"I'm fine," Emmie murmured, wiping her mouth after having used the air sickness bag for what felt like the hundredth time, but was probably only the fifth or sixth.

I crouched down beside of her where she was sitting beside of Shane. "You haven't eaten anything today. How can you still be throwing up?"

"I've been drinking lots of water and Sprite." She sat back, leaning her head against Shane's shoulder as she closed her eyes. "I'm fine, Nik. Really. This is just the air sickness. Not the…" her eyes opened and she met my gaze before looking away again "…baby."

"Why didn't you ask the doctor for those patches you usually wear?" Shane asked.

"I was more worried about other things at the time, Shane." Emmie stood, moving past me without toppling me on my ass. "I have to use the ladies' room."

I climbed to my feet and followed her. To the other people on the plane I must have looked like I was stalking her, and it was probably true. But I was worried about her dammit! Fortunately the plane was full of mostly businessmen, and those few that weren't didn't seem to recognize me and the others. Except for one of the flight attendants who had tried to tempt Shane into a quickie in the bathroom, we had pretty much been left alone.

When she reached the ladies' room, she turned and noticed I was right behind her. "I just have to pee, Nik."

I shrugged. "So pee." With a huff she slammed the door, and I heard the lock click into place. I stood there, listening intently as I tried to hear if she was vomiting again. I didn't hear any retching, but she was in there for so long that I started to wonder if she was alright. Raising my fist to knock, I was stopped by Jesse's hand landing on my shoulder and squeezing. Hard.

"Come on, bro. She's going to be okay." I could tell his words were more to calm me than something he actually believed. The worry in those ever changing eyes of Jesse's told me that he was just as freaked out as I was. "Chill out until we land at least."

With one last look at the closed bathroom door, I followed Jesse back to our seats near Drake. For once Drake wasn't swallowing Jack Daniels like it was water, and I wondered if it was because he wanted to be sober so he could kick my ass too. I knew it was coming from Jesse because I had spent the time being subjected to his threats—more like promises—in between checking on Emmie. I also knew that one word to Emmie and she would step in and make sure Jesse didn't touch me.

I wasn't going to say a word to Emmie about it. I deserved whatever beating Jesse or Drake or Shane dished out. If I was in their shoes I'd be making promises of a broken and bloody body too.

The Rocker That Holds Her

After we landed, some of Emmie's color returned. I wasn't happy until she had kept nearly an entire bottle of Sprite down as we waited for the SUV that Emmie had arranged for us. Once we had the vehicle packed with the smaller luggage and the larger pieces were scheduled for delivery, we all piled into the three row monstrosity of an SUV.

Drake was driving because he handled driving in an unknown city better than the rest of us. He hadn't touched a drop of alcohol all day so I didn't voice a protest. Jesse and Shane climbed into the back and I took shotgun while Emmie stretched out in the middle row. She was still asleep when we pulled up to the beach house.

Emmie didn't even stir as I lifted her into my arms and carried her into the house. I found what I figured was the master bedroom and tucked her into bed. I ached to climb into that big old bed with her but didn't know how she would react come morning. I was acting like a coward, but I was walking through what felt like quicksand with Emmie and didn't know how to get out.

I ended up taking the room directly across from the master suite, leaving my door open so I could listen out for Emmie if she needed something in the night. I bounced onto the big, achingly comfortable bed and was practically asleep before my head hit the pillow.

--

The punch to my gut knocked the air out of me and I bent over, trying to suck in some much needed oxygen.

Coughing, because it was proving to be harder to breathe than I had first anticipated, I glared up at the man that had been my best friend for longer than I could remember. "Good one, bro."

Jesse just glared down at me from his impressive height. "You know what really pisses me off?"

"What?" I wheezed out.

"You're a fucking pussy! For years I've watched you, Nik. I've seen the way that you can't take your eyes off of Emmie. And you know that was okay with me. Out of all of us, you were the good guy. The one that I felt actually deserved her if that was what she decided she wanted. But instead of fighting for her, you hid behind those slutty girls and pushed Emmie away." Jesse punched me in the gut again and I fell to my knees. "Now you got her pregnant and you're still acting like a pussy. Grow a pair, asshole, and make sure she knows that you love her."

He didn't hit me again. He didn't have to. While he walked away, I stayed where I was—on my knees with my entire body aching—after the beating Jesse had just handed out. Jesse hadn't dared hit my face, knowing that Emmie would have torn into him for kicking my ass. But the rest of my body hadn't been off limits. I was going to be hurting for at least a week.

Thankfully Emmie had been sleeping most of the past two days. Otherwise she would have seen Jesse beating some sense into me on the beach. For an all too brief moment I wondered why Shane and Drake hadn't come out to add their two cents and a few punches of their own.

But it wasn't the ass kicking that left me stunned. It was what Jesse had said that was ringing through my ears and left my heart racing. I had been a pussy, a total coward. For years now I had been a silent cry baby and expected Emmie to just assume how I felt about her. I hadn't fought for her.

With a pain-filled groan I got to my feet. Starting right this minute I was going to man up and fight for the only person I wanted to spend eternity with.

I showered, letting the hot water soothe my aching body. The whole time I stood under the spray of the shower I made plans. Growing up, when I wanted nothing more than to be a rock star, I had done nothing but plan: taking private lessons from the music teacher in middle school; convince Drake that he wanted to be a part of my band, because I knew I couldn't do it without him; getting gigs at all the hot clubs while we waited to be recognized as talented.

I had wanted the rocker lifestyle more than anything at the time. Now, I was making plans for the one thing that meant more to me than my own life.

--

I wasn't surprised when I went back down to the beach and found Emmie asleep in the lounger Drake had carried down for her the day before. The big umbrella protected her from most of the sun, but it didn't shade her body from me. She was wearing running shorts and a bikini top that barely held in her tits. Tits that I realized had grown at least a cup size.

Fuck! I had been a total freak for Emmie's tits before, but now I was practically salivating for a taste of them.

Deciding to let her sleep, I walked into the water hoping that the coolness would relieve my sudden raging hard-on before I woke her up. It felt great to relax and not have to worry about what city we were going to end up in the next day. Life on the road had gotten old, and I was ready to settle down and make a home for us.

Making a mental note to call Rich later to find a realtor, I walked toward the shore and Emmie.

She was still sleeping soundly but I was ready to talk, or at least just sit and hold her. Grinning, I shook my wet head. Cool drops of water landed across her body and she jerked awake. Her sunglasses were pushed up and she glared up at me. "You ass!" she exclaimed.

Chuckling, I dropped down beside her on the lounger. She felt deliciously warm against my damp body. "You're freezing. Is the water that cold?"

"Nah, it feels good to me." I stole her sunglasses and placed them over my own eyes. Settling back, I cuddled her closer. "This is nice." When she was comfortable with her head on my chest I told her about wanting to buy a house. "Let's buy a house on the beach somewhere. Not that one…" I nodded toward the house behind us "…but something similar. Bigger."

She seemed surprised. "Really?"

"Yeah. I like the beach and you seem happy here. We can't live on a tour bus and in hotel rooms forever, Em." I glanced down at her still flat stomach. It was mind-boggling to me that she was already four months pregnant and still not showing. Unconsciously, I skimmed my fingers up and down her bare arm. "Would you like to live in Florida or California."

A small smile teased at the corners of her lips. "I don't care."

"Okay, I'll call Rich later and have him find us a realtor. I want us to have our own place before the summer is over. Plus, I want to tell him that the tour for this fall is off. We can't be traveling so much when you are seven months pregnant."

Her head snapped up so fast she nearly clipped my chin. "What? You can't cancel the tour."

"Sure I can. You can't tour with us that pregnant, Em. And I'm sure as hell not leaving you at home like that. Rich will get over it." *In a year or two.* Rich and Emmie didn't get along at all. I was just about fed up with Rich, and it wasn't like we needed him anyway. Emmie had the connections now and the skills to handle any and all our needs as a band. She had been doing it practically from the time she came to live with us. When she turned eighteen, I had made sure that Rich put her on his payroll.

"But, Nik…"

I pushed her glasses up onto my forehead, giving her a look that told her to shut up. "Don't argue with me, Emmie. Nothing you say is going to change my mind. There are more important things than a fucking tour."

Her eyes widened but after a moment she smiled and rested her head back on my chest. "Whatever you say, Nik."

"That's right, woman!" It felt so good to just lie there, talking and holding her. "Let's take a nap. I'm exhausted." Her leg lifted and entwined with mine. Oh, shit. She nearly brushed against my now hard dick. "Then we can go get some dinner." I ran my fingers through her hair, something that had always soothed me as much as it had her. "Just you and me …"

Her head snapped up again. "Like … a date?"

She sounded surprised and excited. I couldn't help but smile, happy that she wanted to go out with me. "Just like a date, baby girl."

Chapter 11

Dreams Don't Come Close

After our nap I went to shower while Emmie got ready. My heart was racing. I don't think I had ever been so nervous to go out with a girl in my life. Of course, it was the first time I was officially going out with a girl. I don't think I had ever actually been on a date my entire life. Even before the band had become a sure thing, I had only cared about fucking. I hadn't wanted to get attached to a girl while I was growing up, so I avoided all forms of commitment.

Emmie had never been the type of girl to linger in the bathroom over how she looked. When she wasn't ready by the time I finished dressing, I went looking for her. I knocked on her bedroom door once before opening it and peeking in. "Hey, babe. Are you ready—" I broke off when I saw what a mess the room was.

I hadn't been in the shower more than twenty minutes. Since then her room looked like it had vomited the contents of her luggage across the room. My eyes caught the sight of one of her bras hanging from the bed post and my cock swelled. Clearing my throat, I forced my eyes back to Emmie. "Em?"

A sob that tore at my heart escaped her. "I have nothing to wear."

It was so unlike Emmie I could only attribute her shift in personality to the pregnancy. I knew I had to tread carefully or she would end up kicking my ass out. "Your room suggests differently, baby. What's the matter?"

"All I have are stupid jeans and most of my shirts have the Demon's Wings logo on them. I don't even own a freaking dress! Not one skirt. All my panties are cotton and my bras are boring!"

I blinked in surprise. "And you want a dress, skirts, and underwear that aren't boring?" My gaze went to the bra again. "That bra hanging from that bed post is pretty fucking hot."

Her glare nearly singed me. "I want something I can wear on our date that you will want to tear off me with your teeth. I want to be sexy!"

How could she not know that she was the sexiest woman I had ever met? Had I been that good at keeping my feelings hidden from her? Calling myself a million different kinds of a fool, I moved to lock her door then returned to her. "Stand up, Em," I commanded.

She just stared up at me curiously, and I grasped her hands and pulled her up. Tenderly, I lifted her chin and forced her to meet my gaze. "Have I ever lied to you, baby girl?" After only a small hesitation she shook her head. "Then listen to me, baby, because I don't want to repeat myself. Okay?" Her teeth latched onto her bottom lip, and I swallowed a groan. I was going to be the one nibbling on that succulent lip before the end of the night. "You are the sexiest woman I have ever met. You don't need more than a pair of ripped jeans, a tattered old shirt, and simple underwear to make me want to strip you with my teeth. Fuck, girl, you make me hard just being in the same room. If I smell your perfume, or whatever the hell it is you wear that makes you smell so damn amazing, I can't walk straight."

When she just remained silent, looking up at me dazed, I went on. "If you want those things, then I will get them for you. Tonight, tomorrow. Whenever you want them. But don't get them unless you want them. Because I want you more now, standing there in that too big shirt and those cutoff jeans than I ever would in some dress or lingerie."

"R-really?" Her voice was shaky and came out a little breathless.

I let my fingers dip into the waistband of her jeans, tracing the silky skin underneath. "Really. So what do you want, Em? Want me to take you shopping?"

"Yes …" I was transfixed as I watched the tip of her pink tongue skim over her bottom lip. "…but, tomorrow."

"Tomorrow?" I was a little disappointed. If she wanted to wait until tomorrow then tonight was off. I had wanted to romance her, show her that I would treat her the way she deserved. "So our date is off?"

When she shook her head I was relieved. "No, I want to skip dinner and fast forward to the kiss goodnight." My dick jerked in my jeans the same time my heart jumped painfully in my chest. "And maybe see how talented you are at stripping me with those teeth of yours."

Maybe it wasn't what I had originally planned, but what better way to show her how much I wanted and cared about her than making love to her? I grinned down at her, feeling like I was a starving animal presented with a feast. "I think I can oblige the lady."

I unsnapped her jeans before reaching for the hem of her shirt. She was still wearing the bikini top, and I sucked in a sharp breath as I stared down at her. The top barely contained the heavy contents of her beautiful tits as her chest rose and fell with each breath. I reached for the string at her neck that held the top up.

Goose bumps popped up on her skin as soon as my fingers brushed over her silky shoulder. Through the material of the bikini top, I watched as her nipples hardened. Carefully, I untied the knot and let the top fall. "So beautiful," I murmured as I skimmed my fingers over her collarbone and down her chest to one hardened nipple.

She was darker there than I remembered, heavier. I cupped her, loving how she fit so perfectly in my hands. A shuddering breath escaped her. "Nik …"

"Shh." I kissed her forehead, inhaling the intoxicating scent of her shampoo. "I'm going to make this so good for you, baby."

I discovered she weighed close to nothing when I lifted her into my arms. Carefully, as tenderly as I could, I placed her in the middle of the bed and followed her down. Her big green eyes were dilated with desire, her breaths coming in little pants, and I hadn't really touched her yet. Fuck, I had been just as blind as she was. Emmie was starving for me just as much as I was for her.

Unable to deny either of us a moment longer, I captured her lips. She tasted like everything I had dreamed. I wanted to kiss her for hours. Cool, trembling fingers fisted my hair, keeping me in place. My hands had a mind of their own as they caressed every part of her I could reach. Her skin was delicately soft, and I was scared of scratching her with my callused hands. But she liked my touch, arching into it as little gasps of pleasure escaped her.

I pulled back from our kiss enough to look down at her trembling body. "Fuck, you drive me wild." I cupped her right breast, gently squeezing until she begged for more.

Switching to the other, I lowered my head and took her nipple into my mouth.

Her cry was loud and drove my need higher. I sucked her harder. Emmie's back arched off the bed, her fingers gripped my arms, nails sinking deep as she let me suckle her beautiful tits. "Ah!" she moaned, making my dick jerk. "Oh gods!"

With one last deep suck, I released her delicious flesh with a small *pop* and kissed down her belly. This close, I could see just the hint of a bump below her belly button. My heart stuttered for a second as the realization truly hit me that my child was growing inside of Emmie. I cupped her little bump and kissed it softly before moving lower.

The top snap was undone leaving the material spread open for me. I kissed the exposed skin, licking and nipping until I reached the top of her zipper. I glanced up at her as I took the zipper between my teeth. Our gazes locked as I lowered the little piece of metal. There was almost no green left in her eyes she was so turned on. I lifted onto my knees and tugged her jeans off before tossing them into the madness Emmie had made of the room with the rest of her clothes.

She was left only in a pair of black cotton panties. With her knees slightly bent and her legs spread, I could see they were damp with her arousal. My fingers shook as I touched the wetness on her left thigh. There had been hundreds of girls spread out before me just like this in the past, but I couldn't remember any of them as I stared down at Emmie.

I lowered my head and kissed each thigh, licking away her arousal. I became an instant addict, her flavor my new drug of choice, as I skimmed my tongue over her damp panties. Her entire body jerked, and she whimpered my name as I lifted one edge so I could taste more of her. Her hips lifted, seeking a deeper kiss.

I latched onto the hem of her panties with my teeth and peeled the material down her thigh until her drenched pussy was completely exposed. I loved that she wasn't completely bare, that even though she kept her beautiful pussy well groomed it still had a line of auburn curls. I combed my fingers through those curls and parted her outer lips with my thumbs to expose the hidden treasure inside.

Her clit bloomed for me it was so swollen with need. I brushed over the bundle of nerves with the tip of my tongue, causing a sob to escape Emmie as she twisted and shook with desire. With my hands on the insides of her thighs, I spread her wider as I sucked on her clit, kissing and tonguing it while she went crazy under me.

"Nik…" My name came out breathlessly. "I'm close… Ah! Nik, please. Nik… NIK!" She screamed my name as she exploded against my tongue. I thrust a finger into her, wanting to feel her clenching around me.

I gave her time to recover, wanting her completely sane when I became a part of her. I watched—loving her, needing her—as she drifted down from the release I had given her. A shy smile teased at her lips as she snuggled against me. "More."

"Whatever you want," I promised and reached to unsnap my jeans. Ten seconds was all I needed to undress before I was lying beside her once again. Her soft body felt amazing against my hard one.

I pulled her body against me, kissing her as I let my hands relearn every inch of her incredible body. Unconsciously, my hand kept going to her hip where the tattoo with my name was. If she was marked with my name, then I wanted to be marked with hers. A drive down to Miami was in order soon. I knew a great tattoo artist that could give me what I had in mind.

The first brush of her fingers over my stomach made all thoughts leave my mind. Her touch was hesitant at first, but when I groaned my approval she grew more courageous. When her fingers drifted lower, touching my aching dick, I nearly wept from the pleasure. I covered her fingers, cupping them around my shaft to encourage her not to stop.

Her grip tightened and I had to clench my jaw to keep from exploding then and there. Her strokes grew bolder. Her fingertips spreading proof of my arousal over the head of my cock, teasing me to the point of madness. With a growl I grasped her waist and rolled us until I was lying on my back and she was straddling my waist.

This was my favorite position. I wanted to watch her, see the desire crossing her face as she rode me. I wanted those tits bouncing while she took me deep into that hot little pussy, over and over again. "Take me inside you, Em."

She lifted onto her knees until she could take the tip of my dick inside of her. The feel of her heat on me made me curse. The first stroke down had me seeing stars it was so good. She was tight, wet, and on fire for me. When she stopped half way I nearly cried out and pulled her the rest of the way down. Concern filled me and I grasped her hips. "You okay?"

Emmie licked her lips. "Yeah ..." She was panting, sweat beading on her forehead. "Just savoring this."

My fingers tightened. "It feels amazing, doesn't it baby?"

"Yes," she breathed, her eyes rolling back into her head as she took another inch of me deeper. "So, so good. Gods, Nik! Ah…"

Her inner walls clenched around my shaft, alerting me to her approaching orgasm. I wanted to feel it so bad. Cupping her with one hand, I used my thumb to rub across her clit, driving her closer to the edge. "Yes!" she cried. "Yes, please."

Her walls clenched around me harder, making my balls tighten as my own release neared. It was mind-numbingly good. I wasn't even completely inside of her, had yet to even thrust my hips once, but I was hanging on the edge of a release that promised to shoot me to the stars. It was too good, too perfect to be real.

The instant I felt her release gushing down my dick, flooding over my balls, I erupted. With a shout of her name, I emptied deep inside of her hot pussy.

Chapter 12

Hope

I woke with the world's most perfect ass snugly resting against my dick. I had one hand full of Emmie's tits and the other over the life we had created together four months ago.

In other words, I woke up in paradise.

When she shifted slightly and her breathing changed I knew that she was awake, and I gave in to the need to kiss her neck. "Morning, baby. How did you sleep?"

"If I said that it was the best night's sleep I've ever had would you believe me?"

Her answer brought a smile to my lips. "Yes. It was one of the best night's sleep I've ever had too."

She turned in my arm. "*One* of the best?"

Her irritation made me even happier. If she was jealous, even a little, then there was hope for us. Biting back a smile, I nodded. "Yep."

Those big, beautiful green eyes narrowed on me. "What were the other ones?"

Despite my efforts to fight it, I couldn't contain my happy grin. "Let me see… a few weeks ago when you crawled in beside me on the bus. When you couldn't sleep last year and we spent the night in my hotel room just talking until I fell asleep…" I shrugged. There were countless other nights that I could remember sleeping peacefully, only because she had been right beside me all night long. "All of them seem to involve you sleeping in my arms."

Her brow relaxed, a sure sign that I was out of danger. "I don't know why I keep you around sometimes, mister."

I laughed, happy to my core, as I gazed down at her. "Let's grab a shower, baby. I'm starving." If we didn't get out of bed now, I knew I wasn't going to be able to keep my hands off her for long. Even after spending most of the night making love to her, I was still hungry for more. I prayed to all of Emmie's gods that I would always want her this much.

I heard her stomach growl and grinned down at her. "How about some bacon?" I loved that she had developed a craving for one of my favorite breakfast foods. Our kid was more like me than Emmie so far, and it made my heart fill with love.

She laughed. "I'm going to end up hating bacon before this is all over."

After breakfast, which we ate alone because the guys were still in bed, I took Emmie shopping. If she wanted sexy new clothes, then I was going to get the pleasure of watching her try them all on. Of course I was pretty clueless as to where to take her, and Emmie was stubborn about not wanting over the top designer brands.

We ended up at the mall. Not my best idea. A truth that became blatantly obvious to me as soon as we stepped into American Eagle. A sales girl that barely looked old enough to be working there screamed, and I felt Emmie jerk beside me. The girl attracted attention and soon I was surrounded by females ranging in age from fifteen to forty.

This was the norm, and I had gotten used to it over the years. Someone recognized me, especially a girl, and everything else stopped. I laughed, more annoyed than flattered, because I had only wanted to spend the day with Emmie.

By the time I untangled myself from the group, I found Emmie had disappeared on me. What the fuck? Why would she just run off on me like that?

Muttering a curse, I pulled out my phone and called her. It rang three or four times before it suddenly went to voicemail, telling me that she had diverted my call on purpose. I glanced around, trying to spot her in the crowd. "Em?" I called her name.

I had searched the entire first floor of the mall before getting the security staff to help. I was going out of my mind. Emmie didn't just go off without a word. If she was mad at me, she wouldn't have wasted a minute in telling me to my face, so I knew there had to be something else wrong. Fear of not being able to find her chilled my heart.

For a brief second I imagined the beating I would get if I had to return home without Emmie. Jesse sure as fuck wouldn't hold back from breaking something valuable this time around, and Drake and Shane would make sure I begged for mercy before finishing me off. But that didn't matter. It was my own sanity I feared for if I didn't find Emmie. I was nothing without her.

The second floor was producing nothing, and I was starting to reach my breaking point. My throat ached and I was fighting both tears and rage. How dare she just wonder off? She wasn't a kid anymore. For fuck's sake, she should act more mature than playing hide and seek with me in a busy ass mall.

The Rocker That Holds Her

Three security guards met me outside of one of the smaller stores and told me they hadn't found her yet. There was the small possibility that she was having lunch on the third floor, which basically consisted of the food court and nothing else, but I knew she wouldn't be up there. Emmie wasn't much on fast foods any more than I was these days.

Still, I was desperate so I turned to follow the men.

"Nik!"

My head snapped around at the sound of Emmie calling my name. Everything around me seemed to stand still for a moment as my eyes zeroed in on Emmie standing inside the store I had just passed. My heart lifted into my throat, and for just a second I felt like I couldn't breathe as I looked at her.

Then I was moving fast. I ran toward her and when I was close enough to touch her I pulled her hard against me. I was trembling from head to toe. "Don't you ever fucking do that to me again!" I practically yelled at her.

Her cheeks were slightly pink, and I could see the hurt and anger in her green eyes. But she just gave me a soft kiss on the cheek. "I figured you were having so much fun with the fan club that you wouldn't even miss me."

Her tone was dismissing, as if the subject bored her. But the way she was standing, with her head at a stubborn angle and her shoulders set in that way that told me she was anything but bored, suggested otherwise. "Were you jealous?" It filled me with both hope and dread at the possibility that she was *that* jealous.

Hope because that told me she had stronger feelings for me than just desire. Dread because I didn't want her to hurt for any reason, ever.

Instead of answering me she turned around to face the girl standing behind the counter. "Thanks for all your help, Beth. Nik, Beth has been so much help today. I spent three grand of your money without even realizing it."

I was surprised and delighted that Emmie had spent so much on herself, but offered the girl a grin. "Thank you, Beth."

The girl must have been incredibly helpful because Emmie pulled out one of the shirts she had bought and scribbled her name on the back with a sharpie before handing the marker to me to do the same. After offering the girl a signed poster, Emmie was ready to leave. I handed the signed shirt over to the cute sales girl and picked up Emmie's bags.

Dammit, I had wanted to watch her try these things on!

--

Emmie ignored me the rest of the day.

Every time I walked into a room she was in, hoping to talk to her about what had happened at the mall, she left. By bed time I was frustrated, annoyed, and a little desperate. I wanted to bend her over my knee and spank her, then make love to her until she was no longer blind to how I felt.

I knocked on her bedroom door before turning the handle. My frustration shot up to an all new level when I found the door locked. Emmie and her fucking stubbornness! "Em, please don't do this." *Don't shut me out. Don't push me away.*

I stood outside her bedroom door until Drake walked upstairs in search of one of his bottles of Jack Daniels. "She kick you out already?"

"Something like that."

"I knew she was smart," he muttered to himself as he walked on down the hall toward his bedroom.

I grimaced. Of my three band brothers, Drake was the only one that seemed to be having trouble with the thought of me with Emmie. It didn't bother me as much as I thought it would. I knew Drake's reasons for not wanting a man like me with the girl that he had spent so many years protecting. And it was only because I knew his reasoning that kept me from feeling like he had just punched me in the gut as hard as Jesse had the day before.

Running my hand through my hair in frustration, I went into my room and slammed the door. Not bothering to shower, I flopped down on my bed and glared up at the ceiling. Time to start working on Plan B.

After finally falling asleep around two that morning, I woke ready to tackle the situation with Emmie. Jesse was camped out in front of the flat screen in the living room watching ESPN.

"Em up yet?'

"Haven't seen her," he answered without looking my way.

Shane was in the kitchen, getting ready for a run. "Want some company?" I asked, needing to work off some of my frustration before I saw Emmie.

Shane raised an eyebrow. "You want to go running with me? On the beach?"

I shrugged. "Seems like a good idea to me."

It fucking wasn't. I had barely ran a mile before my legs felt like they were going to give out. Running on the beach was ten times harder than running on a treadmill. Cursing myself, I stopped in front of a beach house and just sat down. I needed a case of water and a few energy drinks before I was going to be able to stand again.

Shane noticed I wasn't still beside of him and ran back to me. Seeing my sweat covered face, he burst out laughing. "Dude! Not even a mile. You're more out of shape than I gave you credit for."

Unable to catch my breath, let alone tell him to fuck off, I gave him the finger instead and rested my head on my bent knees. It took a good five minutes before I could breathe without panting. By that time we had attracted some attention from the house we had stopped in front of.

Shane let out a whistle, and I knew that there were girls coming our way. Groaning, I reluctantly got to my feet and turned to watch the ladies approach. Tight little bodies in bikinis that just barely covered what needed covering had Shane salivating beside me. All thoughts of his run were now wiped from his mind as his own form of paradise walked toward us.

I wasn't impressed in the least by the girls that used the house as a timeshare. If anything, I was bored as they talked with us for a while. I stuck around only because Shane grabbed my arm when I started to walk away. Not surprisingly, Shane talked all of the girls into coming back to our beach house.

Jesse and Emmie were gone by the time we got back. Drake had just woken up so he had no idea where they went or when they would be back. I didn't even bother to go up to my room and grab my phone. I trusted Jesse now and knew that he didn't want Emmie the way I did. The longer I waited for them to get back, the more stupid my thoughts became. I kept thinking of how jealous Emmie had been the day before and an idea that had nothing at all to do with the plan I had made just the night before started to form.

When I heard the SUV pull into the driveway, I let two of the girls cuddle up to me. For some reason I needed to know for sure if what Emmie had felt the day before came close to how jealous she could make me. Okay, I'll admit it. Maybe I was still stinging a little over the kiss that Emmie and Axton shared and I wanted just a little payback now that I knew she had some feelings for me.

I was an asshole.

I watched Emmie peeking out the living room window and didn't try to untangle the girls who still had themselves pressed up against me like a second skin. I waited until I couldn't see her in the window anymore before I stepped away from them.

Jesse came out a few minutes later, his face a thundercloud as he stepped up beside of me. "Dick move, Nik. Don't make me have to mess up that pretty face."

Guilt washed over me and I sighed. "I'll fix it," I assured him before introducing the two girls that had just been all over me to Jesse. Then I got the hell out of there before I dug myself into an even deeper hole and went inside.

Emmie had locked herself in her room again, and I decided to give her time to cool off before I confronted her. I loved that girl with everything inside of me, but she could really be a stubborn little bitch at times. Of course, I liked that shit.

With ESPN playing in the background, I relaxed on the couch in the living room and surfed the net on my phone as I tried to find the perfect place to take Emmie for dinner the next evening. I needed to take my girl on our official date.

go up to my room and grab my phone. I trusted Jesse now and knew that he didn't want Emmie the way I did. The longer I waited for them to get back, the more stupid my thoughts became. I kept thinking of how jealous Emmie had been the day before and an idea that had nothing at all to do with the plan I had made just the night before started to form.

When I heard the SUV pull into the driveway, I let two of the girls cuddle up to me. For some reason I needed to know for sure if what Emmie had felt the day before came close to how jealous she could make me. Okay, I'll admit it. Maybe I was still stinging a little over the kiss that Emmie and Axton shared and I wanted just a little payback now that I knew she had some feelings for me.

I was an asshole.

I watched Emmie peeking out the living room window and didn't try to untangle the girls who still had themselves pressed up against me like a second skin. I waited until I couldn't see her in the window anymore before I stepped away from them.

Jesse came out a few minutes later, his face a thundercloud as he stepped up beside of me. "Dick move, Nik. Don't make me have to mess up that pretty face."

Guilt washed over me and I sighed. "I'll fix it," I assured him before introducing the two girls that had just been all over me to Jesse. Then I got the hell out of there before I dug myself into an even deeper hole and went inside.

Emmie had locked herself in her room again, and I decided to give her time to cool off before I confronted her. I loved that girl with everything inside of me, but she could really be a stubborn little bitch at times. Of course, I liked that shit.

With ESPN playing in the background, I relaxed on the couch in the living room and surfed the net on my phone as I tried to find the perfect place to take Emmie for dinner the next evening. I needed to take my girl on our official date.

Chapter 13

Open Your Fucking Eyes

It was late when I finally went up to bed. Despite being stressed about Emmie and our future, I had relaxed watching a baseball game and pigging out on the pizza that the guys had ordered for dinner.

I glanced at Emmie's closed door with a feeling of longing making my chest ache. I wanted to be behind that door with her, cuddled up after making love to her for the third time that night. My dick jerked at just the thought of being inside of Emmie's tight little body. Grimacing, I bypassed my bed and went on into the bathroom for a cold shower.

I was still half awake when I heard a vehicle in the driveway. Wondering if Jesse or one of the other guys had come back early, I stood and went to the window. It took me a few seconds to really register what I was seeing and then my heart stopped.

A taxi pulled into the driveway and Emmie was standing there talking to the driver who had yet to get out of the car. The only light was from a street lamp, but I saw her suitcases as if it were plain as day. I hadn't even thought of the possibility of her running away. She had been a part of my life for so long, had stuck with me and the guys through some really horrible shit. But now she was leaving us …

She was leaving *me*!

I turned from the window and ran. If I didn't get to her in time I might never see her again. My heart clenched at just the thought. I nearly fell running down the stairs but somehow kept my footing. I barely paused to unlock the front door and hauled ass.

"Em!" I shouted her name.

She said something to the driver that I couldn't hear because the blood was rushing through my ears. Fear had my adrenaline pumping and I could barely breathe from the way my heart constricted in my chest.

"Stop!" I yelled. "What the fuck are you doing?" She started to get in the back of the taxi but I reached her before she could even get the door closed. My fingers shook as I grasped her arm. I was less than gentle when I forced her to turn and face me. I instantly regretted touching her like that, but my fear in losing her had my mind all kinds of jumbled up. "Where are you going?"

"Away!"

I could actually feel the color draining from my face. Oh fuck. Oh, fuck. Oh. FUCK! "The fuck you are! You aren't leaving. You can't leave." My voice cracked, and I could feel the tears forming as my throat and sinuses started to burn. "Get back in the fucking house!"

"Why?" she challenged me. "Why should I stay here? So you can torment me with all of those skanks? So that you can rub it in my face with what I can never have?" She laughed and the coldness of the sound sent chills down my spine. "Thanks, but no thanks. I'm tired of it all. Tired of seeing the different women flowing in and out of your bed. Tired of dreaming of something I know I can never have."

"What the hell are you talking about?" Had she lost her mind? "There hasn't been anyone in my bed in months! Jesus Christ, Emmie. Are you blind? Can't you see how I feel about you?" Even after our amazing night together two nights ago she still couldn't see how I felt?

Her brow wrinkled and I was too upset to notice how cute she looked. "What feelings?"

Her question gutted me. She was still so blind. I wanted to scream at her to open her fucking eyes. Instead, I closed my eyes, trying to calm myself. "Please, Em. Come back into the house and let's talk. Don't leave, baby. Please don't go."

She didn't say a word and I could actually see the wheels turning in that beautiful head of hers. Emmie was stunned that I had confessed to having feelings for her. Instead of giving her time to make up her mind, I grabbed Emmie's purse. I was only in a pair of boxers and didn't have my wallet, so I grabbed what cash she had and handed it over to the driver.

The man unloaded the cases while I stood there watching Emmie closely, terrified that she was going to make a run for it if I took my eyes off her for even a second. Only after the taxi's taillights had disappeared into the night did I grab her suitcases. "Come on, baby."

I left her cases by the front door. Needing to touch her, I took her hand, tugging her up the stairs. I thought about taking her into her room but knew that I wouldn't get much talking accomplished with the memories of making love to her on that big bed constantly filling my head every time I looked at it. I took her into my room and locked the door.

I gently pushed her onto the edge of my bed and crouched down before her. "Where were you going, Em?" My throat ached from the lump of emotion still choking me.

"Somewhere where there aren't groupies and skanks everywhere I turn around."

I grimaced, regretting even more that I had hurt her today. But with the regret came more hope. "Are they really that upsetting to you? Now, after all the years you have lived with us?" Had I ruined everything today?

Her glare was full of ice. "What do you think? Should I want to have this baby and subject her to all of those sluts on a daily basis? Should I let her see what you are like? The egotistical rocker who has to have all of his adoring groupies hanging off his arm while I, her mother, has to watch from the sidelines?"

Was that really how she saw me? It hurt worse than if she had actually hit me. "That's how you feel? Like you have to watch from the sidelines?" I cupped her face, forcing her eyes to stay locked with mine. "Don't you know that I want you beside me? You and only you."

A very Emmie-like snort escaped her. "That's pretty hard to imagine, Nik. What with those sluts pushing me away from you yesterday. And today with two skanks rubbing against you like they were in heat."

"So you were jealous!" I couldn't help it. I grinned. I was so happy, so excited to know for sure that she cared about me just as much as I cared about her. The sheer joy of it, something I had rarely felt in my life, spilled over and I laughed out loud.

I heard the crack of her hand hitting my cheek before the sting registered. It knocked the smile off my face and I touched the place she had hit. "I'm so glad that you find rubbing those whores in my face so funny. Who the fuck cares that a little piece of my heart dies every time I see it, right?"

"Oh, sweetheart." I shook my head in frustration. "You really need to open those beautiful green eyes of yours." I took the hand that she had slapped me with and kissed the reddened center. "The only reason those girls were in my arms was so I could find out the truth. Yesterday I suspected, but today I confirmed it."

"What are you talking about?" she demanded.

"I had to know if you felt just as deeply for me as I do for you. Em, you have been driving me insane with jealousy. Do you know that I have come close to killing my best friend at least a hundred different times in the past six months alone?"

Those eyes I loved so much widened in surprise. "Jesse? But why would you do that?"

It was time to lay it all out there now. Tell her everything. I sucked in a deep breath for courage. I had never been so nervous in my life. "For the same reasons why I went crazy when you told me you were pregnant, Emmie. I didn't want anyone but me to touch you. You are mine, Em. It's taken me forever to admit that to myself, but when I did I couldn't stand the idea of Jesse or Ax or someone else touching you." I shook my head. "The night Ax took you to the hospital? He called me ten times before I listened to the messages. I had watched you let him kiss you. Fuck, I couldn't see straight I was so jealous. Then I sang that song and expected you to jump into my arms when I walked off stage …"

I broke off with a grimace at the memory of how that had felt. "But you were gone. I went crazy with rage. Stormed off and refused to answer my phone when Axton called the first time. So when I finally listened to one of the messages he left I …" Emmie lying in a hospital bed with an IV and heart monitor attached to her made me swallow hard. "You were so sick and there I was acting like some petulant child because you weren't falling into my arms like I had been dreaming about."

"I didn't stick around long to listen to your song, Nik. I started throwing up when I realized you were…in love." I had to strain to hear the last word.

"Sweet, sweet Emmie," I murmured, leaning forward to brush my lips over her neck. "Still so blind. How can I open your eyes, baby girl? Do you need me to spell it out? Have I been such a fool in not realizing that you couldn't see just what you have done to me?" I licked the spot under her ear I had recently learned was a weakness of hers. "Yes, I am in love. *There is this Ember in my heart that has hold of me and won't let go.*" I sang a line of the song I had written for her.

A tear spilled from her eye and landed on her cheek. She didn't try to wipe it away as it rolled down her flawless cheek and landed on my jeans. I could see that I had finally gotten through to her. That she was really opening her eyes and seeing me for possibly the first time.

"I love you, Em. With everything inside of me, I love you. You are my favorite dream come to life and I never want to let you go." I brushed my lips over her eyes, wiping her tears away with my tongue. "I need you to breathe. You keep the world afloat when everything else is going insane."

Her entire body shook. "I have loved you for so long, Nik," she confessed softly. "You were my dark prince in rusty armor when I was a kid. Now you have become my reason for getting up each morning. The last few years, watching you with a revolving door of one night stands, has slowly killed me. I instantly hate any female that looks at you."

I was surprised that I was still crouched down in front of her. Her confession of loving me back made me weak. I had been just as blind as I had accused her of being. How could I have not seen how much she cared?

"Oh, baby, I'm sorry. I had no idea." I cupped her face. "They didn't mean anything, Emmie. I swear it. They were just something that distracted me from doing what I knew I shouldn't. When you came to live with us I wanted you then. I thought I was turning into some demented pedophile and I hated myself." I still remember how sick I had felt after waking up from that first dream of her. She had been seventeen and I had felt like such a pervert. "Then I realized that it was just you, but that didn't make me feel any better. So I used the other girls to take my mind—and other things—off of what I wanted most."

I grimaced. "The dreams started a few years ago. I would wake up in the middle of the night with my dick so hard, and it would take all of my will power to keep from seeking out the warmth of your arms so I could make my dreams a reality." As I talked to her I couldn't help but trace the lusciousness of her bottom lip. "That's why our night together didn't surprise me. I just brushed it off as another dream."

Her chin trembled. "I thought you didn't know it was me. I hated myself for taking advantage of you like that. But I lived off the memories." Her fingers combed through my hair, tangling in the ends. "That night was more than I could have ever hoped for …"

For one brief moment I thought that maybe I was dreaming again. She was telling me everything I had ever longed to hear. Then her fingers tugged roughly on my hair and the pain told me that this was real. I brushed a kiss over her lips, lingering for a moment to get a better taste. Knowing that she loved me back gave me the feeling that I could take on the world and win. The longer we talked, the more sure I was of what I really wanted.

It was risky asking her now. I knew I was rushing her, and that could always backfire when it came to Emmie. But I couldn't keep from asking her.

I kissed her again. "You aren't going to leave me, are you, Em?"

"No, never."

"And you love me?" I brushed my nose against hers.

"Yes," came her breathy reply.

"Will you marry me, my Ember?" I held my breath as I waited for her answer, playing with her fingers to soothe myself as she seemed to think about her answer.

"Yes," she said as tears spilled from her eyes once again.

At first I was sure I had heard wrong. "Yes?" I repeated.

She nodded. "Yes, Nik."

I pushed her back against the pillows, my mouth already on hers as I tried to show her how happy she had just made me. Emmie was going to marry me!

I tried to go slow but it was hard when all I wanted was to be inside of her. My hands were already stripping her of her jeans and T-shirt. My mouth couldn't make up its mind where it wanted to taste her next as I moved from kissing her neck to sucking on her nipples. Her short nails raked over my scalp as she whimpered in pleasure.

I sat up long enough to tear my shirt off and toss it over my shoulder. "When?" I demanded as I kissed her shoulder. "When will you marry me?"

Emmie stopped pushing my boxers down. "After the baby is born."

I wanted to argue, demand that she start planning our wedding tomorrow, but if she wanted to wait until after our child was here then I would respect that. For a brief, insane second I had the fear that she would change her mind between now and then but forced those thoughts to the back of my mind when she started pulling my underwear off again.

"Oh gods!" Her eyes were glued to my dick as it sprang free of my boxers. "You're perfect."

"Do you want it, Em?" I pushed her back against the pillows and spread her thighs wide. "Do you want my dick inside of you, baby?"

"Yes." Her voice was all breathy with need. "I want you deep, Nik."

I gripped the shaft tightly in my fist and rubbed the tip over her damp folds. Her heat was scalding and I groaned at how amazing it felt. She trembled with each brush of my cock across her sensitive clit, and I was fighting not to erupt then and there. It was almost embarrassing, the way Emmie made me lose control so fast. Not even when I was a teenager had I been so quick to finish.

"I love you, Nik."

Emmie's whispered words were my undoing, and I sunk into her balls deep. Her legs wrapped around my waist, holding me deep inside of her. "Are you okay?" I managed between pants.

"Mm. Don't stop. I need you, Nik."

"Baby!" I pulled half way out and slowly sunk deep, loving the way her walls clung to me like a second skin.

"Harder," she commanded. "Make me come, Nik."

"Fuck," I couldn't hold back as I started to piston my hips, jackhammering into her hard. Her nails raked down my back as she screamed my name over and over again. When I felt her walls starting to convulse, her nails dug into the skin on my shoulder blades, slicing my back open as she came all over my dick.

Chapter 14

Love At First Sight

I had forgotten to shut the blinds. I groaned and turned onto my stomach, using my pillow to cover my head. Sighing, I snuggled deep under the covers.

But I was awake now and memories of the night before had me sitting up in bed. My empty bed…

I frowned, not completely comprehending that Emmie wasn't in bed with me. "Em?" I called out, hoping she hadn't gone far.

"What?" she asked, walking into my room with a towel wrapped around her. Her long auburn hair was wet from the shower. The soft fragrance of lavender and vanilla filled the room, and I sucked in a deep breath, greedy for the scent that was so Emmie.

"Are you going somewhere?" I asked, trying to force my attention on something other than the fact that I had an almost completely naked Emmie walking around my bedroom.

"We both are." She pushed her hair out of her face and sat down on the edge of my bed. "I have an ultrasound this morning and I want you to go with me. It's time you met your daughter."

I reached for her, pulling her down on top of me as I lay back down. "What time is the appointment?"

Green eyes lit with amusement. "Soon. We don't have time for another round, baby."

"Figures." I wrapped a few strands of her damp hair around my fingers. Right now it didn't matter that there wasn't time to make love to her again. I was content just to hold her like this. Fuck, I would have been content if the world decided to shut down and everything else turned to shit. I had everything I would ever want in my arms.

I kissed her long and hard before rolling her onto her back and lifting up on my elbow. "Still love me?"

Emmie raised a brow at me, full of sass. "Pretty sure I still do." She giggled when I glared down at her. After a moment the laughter died and she bit her lip. "Do you still love me?"

"Baby, my love for you isn't going to change overnight." I brushed another kiss over her lips. "Or ever. No one is ever going to hold my heart like you. Understand?"

She nodded but I saw a flash of uncertainty in her eyes before she pulled my head back down for another kiss. My body was begging for another round of lovemaking, but Emmie was already pushing me off of her as I reached for her towel.

"I have to get dressed and you need a shower."

"You can't kiss a guy like that and just walk off, woman!" I called after her and was rewarded with the sound of her giggling again.

An hour later we were in an exam room waiting on the doctor and the ultrasound tech to come in. Emmie was sitting up on the table in a gown the nurse had given her and nothing more. To tell the truth I was nervous as hell and had no idea why. I had the picture that Emmie had been given from a few days before still in my wallet. I hadn't looked at it much, but the few times I had, I had memorized every inch of the grainy picture.

To distract myself from my nervousness, I kissed Emmie as often as she would let me. Fortunately for me that was often. Unfortunately, I was rock hard and she wasn't going to let me ravish her any time soon. I knew because I had already asked. Twice.

Her lips were swollen from my last kiss, and she licked at the bottom lip, seeming to savor my taste. "Will you be good?" she laughed, something that she had been doing a lot of this morning. "I'm not going to have sex with you when the doctor could come in any minute." Her soft hands pushed at my chest with barely any force, her smile making my heart skip a beat as I watched her. "Nik…"

I stuck my bottom lip out in a pout. "One more kiss?"

Big, green eyes sparkled with happiness. "Okay, just one more." Her arms slid up my chest and her fingers combed through my hair as she pulled my head down.

Yeah, it was official. I was completely addicted to this woman's mouth. Groaning, I thrust my tongue inside, deepening the kiss. Scorching heat greeted me and my hands gripped her hips through the ridiculously thin material of her gown in an attempt to keep from touching her more intimately.

The kiss might have lasted for another hour if there hadn't been a knock on the door. I heard it before Emmie could even comprehend what was going on and reluctantly stepped back from her. I was just turning around when the door opened and the doctor came in with a younger woman behind her.

"Good morning, Ember," the doctor greeted Emmie before zeroing her gaze in on me. "Umm, and you are?"

"Nik Armstrong, ma'am." I offered her my hand. "I'm the daddy."

Her eyes widened and then she smiled. "Great, I always like meeting the father if possible. But since you couldn't be here yesterday it was nice that Jesse was able to come with Ember. That's a pretty nice friend you have there."

I grinned, sensing that the lovely doctor might have developed a crush on my best friend. "Yeah, he's pretty amazing."

The doctor turned her attention back to Emmie. "Is your bladder full?"

Emmie grimaced. "Pretty full."

"Good. We can see the baby better that way." After introducing the tech, the doctor helped Emmie lie back and produced a blanket which she spread over Em's legs before pulling up her gown. "I promise this won't take too long. We just have to get measurements and I want to confirm your due date."

I felt like I was in the way. The tech was busy punching information into her machine while the doctor continued to mess with Emmie to get her comfortable. I stood off to the side, aching to at least hold Emmie's hand. My heart was racing and my palms were sweating. I was terrified.

The more I thought about the baby, the more freaked out I became. I had had a lousy father and there had never been anyone to ever show me how to be a good one. I was going to ruin this kid, I just knew it. She was going to think I was the worst dad in the world because I was such a douche bag.

The lights were dimmed and I didn't even notice. I heard the three women talking but couldn't tell you a word they said. I was trying to keep my cool, at least pretend for Emmie's sake that I was okay.

The voices hushed all of a sudden as the room filled with a strong galloping noise. I frowned, focusing my attention on the screen where the tech was fiddling with nobs and buttons. The galloping was hypnotizing, and I found myself stepping closer to see what was making that oddly beautiful noise.

Like the picture Emmie had given me, it took me a moment or two to focus on what it was supposed to be. But after a minute I saw the outline of a hand as it swung back and forward as if waving at me. Then came the leg and of course the foot as it kicked out at some imaginary ball. My breath caught as I continued to watch my daughter on the screen.

"Everything looks good so far, Ember," the doctor said as she pointed at the screen. "The baby is a good size and is measuring perfectly for your due date. Heart is strong and she looks very active. You should be able to feel her soon."

I listened intently without taking my eyes off the ultrasound screen. The tech moved again and I lost the view I had of the baby's leg and foot. But when she moved out of my way it was to find the head instead. I felt tears burning my throat and had to blink as they filled my eyes as well. My little girl looked like she was smiling as she looked back at me on the screen.

"She's beautiful."

"Yes, she definitely is," Emmie agreed and reached for my hand. "You're going to be a great daddy, Nik."

Before I could stop them my tears spilled over. Emmie knew me better than anyone in the world. I might have thought I was hiding how freaked I was, but she had known anyway. "You think so?" I whispered, wiping at a few tears as they rolled down my cheek.

"No, I know so." She smiled up at me lovingly, making her that much more beautiful. "I love you, Nik."

Not caring that we had an audience, I bent and brushed a kiss over Emmie's lips. It wasn't the kind of kiss I had been giving her before the doctor had come in—one that begged her to let me take her to bed. This kiss had nothing to do with passion and everything to do with how much I loved Emmie... and our daughter.

First Date

By the time we got back to the beach house the guys had gotten home. Emmie made lunch, and we ate in front of the television watching the DVD of the ultrasound that the doctor had given us before leaving her office.

It didn't surprise me that my band brothers wanted to watch the video. It did catch me off guard a little when Jesse started to tear up. My best friend was a big old softie underneath all that scary rocker aggressiveness. Shane made a few wise cracks about the baby, but I could tell he was just as affected as Jesse was. Drake seemed the most apprehensive about it all, but he couldn't keep his eyes from getting glassy when the baby stuck her finger in her mouth and kicked out like she didn't have a care in the world.

If one of our fans had seen all of us, they would have dropped dead with shock, or maybe of laughter. The big bad boys of Demon's Wings just didn't come across as emotional pansies. But really, with the evidence of Emmie's pregnancy waving back at us on the huge flat screen, that was what we were.

When the DVD was over I urged Emmie to take a nap. She looked beat and I hadn't let her get anywhere near enough sleep the night before. As soon as I had her tucked into our bed in the master bedroom, I started working on the plans I had come up with the day before. It didn't matter that we had sorted through the majority of our problems the night before.

Emmie deserved to be wooed. Starting tonight I was going to make sure she got everything she deserved.

I was just finishing up my shower when Emmie walked into the bathroom. She was cursing a blue streak, and I stuck my head out of the shower to watch as she rushed toward the toilet. She didn't seem to notice me as she sat down and then moaned in pleasure. I frowned, concerned. "You okay, baby?"

She grimaced. "It's never felt so good to pee before in my life." She glared at me. "Stop looking at me like that! I'm trying to use the bathroom."

Chuckling, I turned away, rinsing the last of my bodywash away. When the toilet flushed I lost my chuckle as the water turned scalding for a moment. "Em!"

I heard her giggling as she went back into our bedroom, making my grin return in full force as I turned off the water and reached for a towel. The sound of that woman's laughter would always make me smile.

Emmie was snuggled under the covers again when I entered the bedroom. She looked content and still a little sleepy. I ached to climb into bed beside of her and spend the rest of the day making love to her, but I had plans that I intended to follow through with.

I walked over to the closet that I had hung my clothes in while Emmie was still sleeping. "Grab a shower, baby girl." I told her as I pulled out a pair of slacks. I only had three pairs in my entire wardrobe. I fucking hated slacks, but the restaurant I was taking Emmie to tonight wasn't the type of place that accepted jeans and a T-shirt as appropriate attire. "Then put on one of those sexy outfits you bought yesterday."

She yawned. "Why?"

I didn't turn to face her because I knew that I wouldn't be able to stop myself from joining her in bed. "It's a surprise."

"I'm not a fan of surprises, Nik."

I grinned as I pulled a white T-shirt over my head and reached for my dark gray dress shirt. "Guess you will just have to deal, baby."

A pillow hit me in the back, and I laughed out loud but still didn't turn to face her. "Hurry up," I urged as I bent down to get my boots. "You only have about thirty minutes before the car gets here."

"Car? What car?" she demanded.

"I might have gotten a limo for tonight." I had a vision of making love to Emmie on the ride home tonight. With her spread out on the long back seat and my head between her legs as I licked her toward orgasm after orgasm. My dick swelled at just the thought and I had to readjust myself so that I didn't split the crotch seam of my slacks.

"Thirty minutes!" She yelped and I heard her jumping out of bed. "You are such an ass. You can't expect me to get ready in thirty minutes."

Her distressed tone had me finally turning to face her. "Why not?" I had lived with Emmie for over six years now. It never took her longer than ten minutes to get ready for anything. She wasn't like most girls who spent hours in front of the mirror before starting the day.

"Because…" She grunted. "Just because, Nik!" Emmie went into the bathroom, slamming and locking the door behind her.

I sighed. Now she was mad at me. What a great way to start our first date.

Terrified of making her angrier than she already was, I went downstairs to wait for her. Jesse was standing at the stove stirring something that smelled incredible. His eyes widened when he saw me. "Where are you going?"

I shrugged, pulling a beer out of the fridge. "I'm taking Em out to dinner."

"Wow, look at you. Getting smart and shit." He grinned and turned back to whatever he was cooking. "So I guess you won't be eating any of my hamburger helper."

"Is that what that is?" I crossed over to the stove to stand beside him and looked down at the pan he was working on. Macaroni noodles, hamburger, thick cheese, and what looked like some green onion and red peppers were added to the mix. "Dude, that looks awesome. Save me some for later."

"I'll try, bro."

"I'll bring you home a slice of cake or something." I wasn't above bribing. My stomach growled and I was tempted to starting eating from the pan right then and there.

"Fine. I'll make another batch later, just for you." Jesse rolled his ever-changing dark eyes at me. "I want some chocolate cake."

"You got it."

Emmie still hadn't come down by the time the limo pulled up in the driveway. I opened the front door to wave at the driver, letting him know that we wouldn't be long when I heard heeled footsteps coming down the stairs behind me. Turning around to see if Emmie was ready to go, I froze at the sight before me.

To me Emmie was sexy in a pair of baggy pajamas and one of my old shirts. My breath caught in my throat as I took in the beautiful vision that was walking toward me: knee high, stiletto, black boots; a black dress that fell just short of mid-thigh with a modest neck line. Her hair was down, curled around her shoulders and shining. Make-up made those incredibly big green eyes stand out in her perfect face.

My tongue felt like it was glued to the roof of my mouth, and I struggled to form words as she stepped off of the last step and twirled around, showing off the back of her dress. It dipped down to the small of her back, showing off her creamy complexion and slender shoulder blades.

The smile she gave me told me she was over being mad at me, but I was still standing there staring at her like an idiot. "How do I look?"

"I…" I cleared my throat. "Wow… You… I… Wow."

Her giggle did something to my stomach. I was sure there were butterflies flying around in there. "That good, huh?"

"Fuck, Em." Jesse came from the back of the house and saw her standing at the front door with me. "You look hot."

"Thanks, Jess." She stood on tiptoe and kissed him on the cheek before turning back to me. "Are we ready, Nik?"

I shook my head, trying to clear it of the desire she had fogged it with. "You look beautiful, Emmie."

Chapter 15

Jealousy. What A Bitch

A week went by that was full of complete bliss where Emmie and I were concerned. I couldn't ever remember being so happy. Each morning I woke up with Emmie snuggled against me and made love to her until she begged for mercy and something to eat, which had to include something with bacon. The rest of the day was spent hanging out down on the beach or in front of the television with the guys. I took her out every evening, whether to dinner or a movie or just dessert—again with the bacon. Then I brought her home and made love to her until we were too exhausted to move.

Now we were sitting out on the deck. Jesse was lying on a lounger beside me and Emmie was snuggled up on my lounger with me while Drake snored soundly across from us. I was content, close to falling asleep and loving life.

Of course Emmie's phone kept vibrating every five minutes. She had turned the ringer off to keep from disturbing me, but she was texting with someone and the vibrations were starting to get annoying. Yawning, I picked the phone up off my stomach where she had placed it after the last text. "Who are you talking to?"

She shrugged. "Axton."

I tried not to stiffen, tried not to let the images of Emmie kissing my friend fill my mind. Of course it happened anyway. My hand fisted around her phone before I relaxed it enough to look down at the screen and the new text. My eyes narrowed when I read his message. "He is *not* coming here!"

Emmie raised her head, a frown creasing her forehead. "Of course he is."

"No, Em. He fucking is not coming. I don't want him here." I carefully untangled her from around me and stood. I was trying to stay calm, not act like a jealous asshole. But the more I thought of Axton Cage close to my girl, the more I saw red. "He has no business here."

"What the hell is your problem?" she demanded. "Ax is our friend. If he wants to take time out and come visit us he can."

"Friends? He had his hands all over you more than a week ago, Em!"

Green eyes narrowed dangerously on me. "He kissed me. Big deal. He was just messing around. We both know he didn't mean anything by it."

"That's bullshit and you know it." I raked my hands through my hair. "He has a thing for you. Everyone freaking knows it. Even Brie." Gabriella Moreitti hated Emmie just as much as Em hated her because of it.

My back was turned to her as I tried to calm down enough to keep from punching something. Of course it didn't help, so I didn't see the look on Emmie's face, didn't see the hurt and anger that filled her green eyes. I was lost to everything but my own jealousy as I glared out at the Gulf.

"Emmie?" Jesse's voice was full of concern, and I turned to glance at my friend. His eyes were on Emmie, who was still sitting where I had left her. "Emmie, deep breaths."

Tears were pouring down her cheeks as a silent sob had her catching her breath. I was so startled to find her like that my legs nearly buckled. "Em?"

She sucked in a deep breath and a broken sob escaped her, waking Drake. "You have a lot of fucking nerve." Scrubbing a hand over her face, she stood. "One stupid, innocent kiss and you act like I committed adultery. Fuck you, Nik. And fuck precious *Brie* too. Oh, wait. You already did that!"

"What?" I blinked, unsure I had heard her right. "What did you say?"

"You fucked Gabriella! Don't act all innocent. She told me all about it just days after it had happened while we were still in Australia last year. You think that was fun for me? Having one of your fuck buddies tell me the details?" Her phone was clenched in her hand, but she used it as a missile and threw it at my head. "So you can get over Axton because I had to get over Gabriella."

She walked away from me, tears still pouring down her face while I just stood there. Too stunned to do more than stare after her. I had absolutely no idea what she was talking about and it only made my head hurt to try and comprehend it all.

Sex with Gabriella? Had she lost her mind? I didn't even like the little Italian spitfire. Sure she was hot, smoking hot at that. But Axton had hooked up with Gabriella not long into the tour and that had meant hands off in my book. Not that I would have touched her if they hadn't. By that time Emmie had invaded my head to the point that I couldn't think straight, and the few girls I had been messing around with had reminded me of her.

"Well that explains a lot," Jesse muttered.

Drake groaned and turned over on his lounger. "I'm surprised that Em didn't scratch her eyes out when Gabriella told her that."

I glared at my two friends. "Did she really just accuse me of sleeping with Brie?"

Jesse sighed. "Dude, if you want to keep your man parts, I suggest you drop the little nickname that Ax gave Gabriella. That isn't going to win you any points with Em. And to answer your question, yes. I had suspected something like this at the time, but Emmie would never tell me for sure or not."

"There was a rumor going around that you had bagged the little Italian." Drake shrugged, reaching for his half empty bottle of Jack Daniels that was sitting on the deck beside his chair. "I didn't pay any attention at the time, what with her being with Axton."

I groaned. "So she really does think I slept with Br—Gabriella?"

"You mean you didn't?" Drake questioned, taking a pull from his bottle.

"No!"

"Dude, chill out. I believe you." Drake grimaced. "It's Emmie you have to convince."

It seemed like all I was doing was cursing as I threw a few more at my friends and headed into the house after Emmie. Of course she had locked herself in our bedroom. I stood there glaring at the offending door that stood between me and the woman I loved. It might as well have been a thousand foot wall because until Emmie was ready, I wasn't going to get through it.

I tapped lightly and like I had expected, I didn't get a response. "I love you, Emmie," I called to her. I waited in vain for her to scream at me through the door, anything. Nothing came and I reluctantly left her.

Why had Gabriella lied to Emmie about the two of us having sex? Had it been because Gabriella sensed what I had always sensed? That Axton Cage was half in love with Emmie? I had suspected it for years, and it wasn't just my imagination. When I had been so jealous of Jesse, part of me had known that it was just my possessiveness and jealousy rearing its ugly head. But with Axton there was definitely something there.

I couldn't really blame the man for having feelings for her. Not really. Emmie was amazing. She was strong and brave. She had her head on straighter than most women twice her age. She was sassy and feisty and so, so very beautiful.

There wasn't any other reason I could think of that Gabriella could have had to fill Emmie's head with lies. But whatever her reason, that didn't mean I could condone them. Her toxic lies had poisoned my relationship with Emmie and I hadn't even known.

Grimacing, I stomped back downstairs and out onto the deck where Drake and Jesse were still seated, quietly watching the water hitting the beach and rolling back out. I had left my phone out here so I snatched it up and pulled up my contacts. Axton's information was near the top and I hit connect.

It rang three times before my friend answered. "Still pissed at me?" He sounded amused but I could tell that he really was upset.

"We need to talk, Ax."

"Is this about me coming out there in a few days?"

"Yes. No… No, this isn't about you coming. Actually, it would be better if you came today." I was pretty sure that Axton's presence was the only thing that was going to help me convince Em that Gabriella and I had never happened.

"Ah, does Nikki miss me that much?" Axton taunted, laughing. "Sure, man, I'll grab the first flight out."

…Emmie…

I wasn't sure how long I cried. An hour, maybe even a full day. My head was throbbing by the time my tears dried, and I fell asleep for a few hours. When I woke up, the headache was a dull ache but my heart was still hurting. I let out a shaky sigh and glared off into space.

I had thought I was over the whole Nik and Gabriella thing. Of course with my hormones in ten different directions thanks to being pregnant I had made a liar of myself. I wasn't sure if I would ever fully get over Nik having slept with Gabriella.

I could still see the look in that little bitch's eyes as she walked toward me the year before. I could still hear the amusement in her voice as she had said the words that had been like a physical punch to the stomach.

"You should have told me Nik was so talented with his tongue," the beautiful Italian musician had said, her brown eyes alight with laughter. "He really takes care of his women."

Up until that moment I had been undecided if I liked Gabriella Moreitti or not. I had watched her for a while and noticed both positive and negative things about her that could have tipped the scale either way. She was talented, could rock hard, and didn't back down from anything. All pluses. She was also vain, vindictive, and a snob. Not pluses. But I had promised Axton that I would reserve judgment for a while because he had liked her.

I was sure all women had a sixth sense when it came to another woman's weaknesses. I had four, and only one of them could actually break my heart into a million pieces. Gabriella must have known that and had shattered me almost completely the day she told me how good of a lover she found Nik to be.

In that moment Gabriella Moreitti had become public enemy number one in my book. I hated that bitch with everything inside of me. If Jesse hadn't come along and stepped between me and the little Italian violinist, I was sure I would have scratched her pretty eyes out of her beautiful face.

I couldn't understand how Nik could be so upset over a little kiss between me and Axton, a man that was nearly as close to me as Jesse, Drake, and Shane. He had no right to try to put up walls between me and Axton when I should have been the one doing that so he wasn't around Axton's girlfriend so often.

Rubbing a hand over my tear-stained and swollen face I headed into the bathroom and showered. It was dark outside, telling me I had slept for more than seven hours. The steam from the hot shower made me feel just a little better, but I was also starting to feel stupid. I had no right to be mad a Nik for something he had done when we weren't even together. He said he loved me now, and that was all that mattered.

I dressed in a pair of sweat pants and one of Nik's shirts. My stomach was growling and the craving for a bacon sandwich was making my mouth water. When I walked downstairs I could hear Jesse, Drake, and Shane talking in the living room. A Boston Red Sox game was on and they were losing. Shane wasn't happy.

Not feeling up to facing them after my humiliating outburst earlier, I bypassed the living room and took the long way to the kitchen. To my surprise there was some freshly fried bacon in a bowl, the grease draining onto a folded paper towel. Not questioning my good luck, I grabbed the bread and the jar of mayo from the fridge.

I stuffed a crispy piece of bacon into my mouth as I added some sliced tomato to my sandwich. My mind was completely on making my sandwich, eager to satisfy the baby's cravings.

"How are you feeling?"

I jumped at the sound of a voice I definitely hadn't been expecting. Frowning, I turned to find Axton standing by the back door. "What are you doing here?" I demanded with a smile.

"Nik asked me to come." He shrugged, leaning against the wall by the door, watching me with that sly grin of his. The thing I loved most about Axton was that I never knew when he was being serious or not. That was also the thing I hated most about him. You had to truly know him before you could figure out his tells. He seemed laid back and carefree, but I knew that he was just the opposite.

Over the years, as we had become closer friends, he had told me a little about his past. He came from a crazy rich family that had never supported his love and passion for music, especially rock. His mother had had her own plans for him. Axton would become a lawyer, take over the family business, and marry a girl that his mother thought was appropriate. Not the type of person to just let someone dictate his life, Axton had simply told her to go fuck herself and had signed on with Rich Branson the very next day with OtherWorld. I wasn't sure, but I didn't think that Axton had talked to his mother since.

I wiped some of the bacon grease from my fingers, trying to digest what Axton had just said. Nik asked him to come? But Nik had been completely against Ax coming at all. "Where is Nik?" I hadn't heard him in the living room earlier.

"Sitting out on the beach, drinking a beer." Axton took a step toward me. "So Brie slept with Nik. Not."

I blinked, confused by what he had just said. "What?"

He grimaced. "He didn't sleep with her. Brie doesn't even like Nik, as far as I know. Besides, Brie isn't the type for one night stands. It took me freaking forever before she had sex with me. She's old school Italian like that. Well, I guess not old school. She wasn't a virgin waiting for her wedding night, but still."

"Ax…"

"Nik loves you, Emmie." His jaw tensed as he said the words. "More than anyone else ever can or will. I'm not telling you this because he asked me to. He did, but that's not why I'm doing it. I'm telling you because you are probably my best friend in the fucking world, and I want you to be happy. Nik didn't have sex with Gabriella. She's a bitch, and I'm not sure why I even put up with her. She lied to you because she thought that I was into you, and that made her mad. So she hurt you to pay you back for something you never did." Axton grimaced, running his fingers through his hair in a very un-Axton kind of way. Ax didn't get frustrated to the point that he started tugging at his hair often.

The ache in my heart eased a little. "They really didn't have sex?"

"Nope, I don't think they have even been alone together."

Tears filled my eyes and I turned away from Axton before he could see them. I wasn't sure why I was crying again. Maybe it was because I felt like my heart had had a deep crack healed by Axton's words. Maybe it was just because I was on some kind of hormonal overload because I was pregnant. Either way I hated crying, but that was all I seemed to be able to do!

Strong hands touched my shoulders tenderly. Axton had moved to stand behind me. When I didn't move he kissed the top of my head. "Go talk to Nik. Put him out his misery. Poor bastard is all kinds of fucked up right now."

Chapter 16

One Step Forward…

The half-moon was shining bright over the Gulf Coast. I frowned up at the sky, full of stars and hope for those that wished on those twinkling little diamonds. I was almost desperate enough to wish on one myself tonight.

Emmie had been in her room all day. I had gone to check on her a few times and the room had been so quiet inside that I had figured she was sleeping. Each time I turned away from the door that led into our shared room my heart had felt a little heavier. When Axton had finally arrived, I breathed a little easier, but I still couldn't shake my unease.

Way too many *What Ifs* kept flashing through my mind. What if Emmie didn't believe me, or even Axton about Gabriella? What if she couldn't move on from this? What if I lost her?

My hands shook as I thought of what my life would be like without Emmie in it. My throat grew dry, and I took a long swallow from my Corona to ease some of the tightness. It didn't help so I took another drink.

"It's a beautiful night out."

My head jerked up at the sound of Emmie's voice. I had been so lost in my own misery that I hadn't heard her approaching. She was standing right beside my lounger, looking up at the sky with the slightest hint of a frown on her beautiful face.

"Yeah. Beautiful." But my eyes were on her, not the sky. Nothing was more beautiful to me than Emmie.

She stood there for the longest time just staring at the water and the star filled sky. I didn't mind the silence. Simply having her next to me eased some of the tightness that had been clenching my heart all day long. If she was down here with me now, that had to be a good sign.

"I woke up feeling stupid," she said in a voice so quiet that I had to strain to hear her. "I don't have any right to be mad at you for something that happened more than a year ago."

"Em…" I tried to stop her, to explain that there was nothing for her to be mad about in the first place, but she stopped me by turning to face me.

Even in the dim light of the half-moon and the lights coming from the beach house behind me I could tell that she had been crying. Her big green eyes were still puffy and her face still a little pink. "Axton told me that Gabriella lied. I'm sorry, Nik. I've made such a mess of things lately."

I reached for her. Taking her hands, I pulled her down onto my lap and did the only thing I really could do. I kissed her. Her lips were salty from her tears, but still the sweetest things I had ever tasted in my life. I let go of her hands and tangled my fingers in her hair. I was helpless to control my groan when she opened her mouth and let me inside her hot mouth.

The kiss lasted forever, but nowhere near long enough. When I pulled back I was reluctant to let her mouth go but knew that we needed to talk. I kissed her lips one last time, savoring her taste on my tongue. "I love you, Em."

Her chin trembled. "I love you, too."

Every time she said it, every time I heard those words leave her mouth, my heart stuttered in my chest. "I wish you would have said something about Gabriella, baby. There was never anything going on between us. Never. By the time she came on the scene I was barely functioning because I wanted you so much. Even if she had wanted something, I never would have been able to touch her."

"We've both been idiots. We could have been together long before now if we had opened our eyes." She sighed and buried her face in my neck. "I've loved you for so long, Nik. Even now it's kind of hard to get my head around the fact that I finally have you."

I pressed a kiss to her cheek. "I know. It's the same for me."

Slowly she raised her head. "About that kiss with Axton …" I tensed, the images of her kissing my friend making my stomach turn and my heart squeeze. But I didn't say anything. I needed to hear what she had to say. "It didn't mean anything, Nik. I swear. I don't know what it was for him, but for me it was just him playing around. Axton is my friend. It would never be more than that."

"I know, Em." I pulled her head down onto my chest. "I know." I honestly believed that for her it had only been Axton teasing, just as I believed that for Axton it had been so much more. But I wasn't going to think about that. It would only drive me crazy and ruin my friendship with Axton.

We sat like that for a good hour, neither of us talking as we held on tight to each other. The sound of the water hitting the beach and rolling back out was soothing. I was sure that as long as I had Emmie in my arms nothing else would ever matter again.

Emmie sat up so suddenly her head almost knocked my jaws together. "Oh my gods!" she whispered.

I rubbed at the sore spot on my chin where her head had connected. "Are you okay?"

"I think…" She giggled as she held her hand over her stomach. "There it is again."

"What?" I demanded, concerned.

"The baby. I just felt her. She's kicking up a storm in there." She grasped my hand and laid it over her stomach where she had just been touching. "Right here."

I smoothed my hand over her slight bump, and she pressed my hand a little tighter against her. At first I couldn't feel anything and felt disappointed, but then Emmie shifted a little and I felt it, just a little flutter under my fingertips. My heart contracted and my throat grew tight. "Was that her?" I asked in an emotionally rough voice.

"Yeah, that was her." Emmie laughed. "This is so amazing, Nik. I was scared I wasn't ever going to feel her kicking, and now she's starting to use me as a punching bag."

I grabbed Emmie's waist and lifted her until her stomach was level with my mouth. Her hands gripped my shoulders to steady herself, but she should have known that I would never have dropped her. Grinning, I pressed a kiss against her stomach where I had felt our child moving. "I can't wait to meet you, little girl," I whispered against Emmie's flesh. "I can't wait to show you the world."

Emmie's hands moved from my shoulders to my hair, tangling in the thickness as she held me against her for a moment. Then she was pulling away, straddling my waist. "Make love to me, Nik."

"Here? Now?" I was already reaching for the snap on my jeans, but I had to be sure that this is what she wanted.

"Yes," she breathed, pulling my head down for a kiss that had me losing all my reasoning skills.

The beach was private so I wasn't worried about anyone stumbling upon us. As for my band brothers and Axton, I didn't give a fuck if they saw us. I stripped Emmie's shirt off of her, relishing in the sight of her alabaster skin in the pale moonlight. I was sure that I was never going to see a sexier sight.

When she was free of all of her clothes, I pulled my dick from my jeans and positioned Emmie over me. I had never in my wildest dreams thought I would get to make love to this woman, and now here I was loving her on the beach as if we were pagans. Out of all the freaky shit I had done in my life, this blew my mind.

Neither of us could stop the whimpers of pleasure that escaped us as I slipped into her tight, hot, little body. She felt so damned good I knew I wasn't going to last long. It was almost embarrassing how quickly Emmie could get me to the edge of exploding. Fortunately, she always got me hard again as soon as I did.

I was still trembling with the effects of my first release, but I was stone-hard as she kept riding me. She was wild in my arms, a true tempest as she let herself go to the pleasures that I could give her.

"Nik!" She cried my name as I felt her inner muscles clamp around my shaft, urging me toward my second release in as many minutes. "Gods, Nik. I love you so much."

Some Shit Hits The Fan!

The house phone was ringing.

That should have been my first clue that something was up. No one knew the number at the beach house here. If anyone important needed to reach us they could easily get hold of us on our cell phones, and if it was overly urgent they knew to call Emmie.

I ignored the annoying sound of the phone. That particular noise had always been like nails on a chalkboard for me. It seemed like nothing good ever happened when I heard a phone ringing.

After a few more rings someone answered the insistent thing and I went back to reading over the last few lines of the latest song I had been working on. I was so lost in what I was doing that I didn't notice how quiet it had suddenly gotten inside the house. The sun was shining down on me and I didn't have a care in the world.

"NIK!"

My head shot up at the sound of Emmie screaming my name. I knew that tone. It wasn't a "Nik, I need help" scream, more like a "Nik, your fucking ass is in trouble." I gripped my pen and wondered what the hell I had done now.

It had been a few days since we had cleared the air about the whole Gabriella issue. Axton was still hanging around, but I knew he was ready to head back to the West Coast. Now that we had decided to find a house on the

West Coast too, Axton was pretty happy. We were all Axton had really. His family were all dickheads and he didn't claim them, and even if Emmie wasn't like his sister, I knew that he needed her just as much as my band brothers needed her.

The door behind me slid open and Emmie came out, the house phone in her hand. She swung it around like it was a weapon and I bit down on the inside of my cheek to keep from grinning. That would only raise the temperature of her rage and send that pot to a full on boil. See? I was getting smarter.

"What's wrong, baby?" I asked, both cautious and curious.

"Rich let it slip about the baby. Now every tabloid this side of the globe has the story and is running it." She tossed the phone on the table in front of me. "I'm the most hated female on the planet right now. The stories range from how I trapped you into asking me to marry you to how I am secretly your sister and that the baby is going to have webbed toes and a sixth finger on each hand."

A snort of laughter escaped me before I could stop it, and Emmie glared down at me. But through the anger I saw the real problem. Emmie was still feeling insecure and I could see the doubt hiding in the depths of those big green eyes I loved so much. "You didn't trap me into anything, baby. We both know that you couldn't get me to cross the street unless I really wanted to. Marrying you, that's a dream I thought would never come true. Don't worry about the tabloids. That will all blow over in a few weeks."

Some of the anger drained out of her, and I reached out, pulling her down onto my lap. "No pouting." I kissed her lips, sucking her pouty lip into my mouth and savoring that taste that always went straight to both of my heads. "I love you."

She sighed and leaned her head on my chest. "I love you, too." She sighed again. "You know it was Rich that tipped them off to get back at me, right? He blames me for you refusing to tour anytime soon."

I grimaced. "Yeah, I know."

Rich was really starting to get on my nerves. He had been an awesome manager up until Emmie had come on board. Once she had started taking over his responsibilities, he had taken the easy way out. Jesse and I had to make him start paying Emmie for all the hard work she did. He had turned his attention to some of the smaller bands that he managed and still made a hell of a profit off of us. Our contract was up for renewal in a little over a year and a half, and I was sure that I wasn't going to sign a new one when it was up.

"Don't worry about Rich either, Em. We're on vacation, and I forbid you to worry about anything but the baby. Well other than making love to me at least twice a day."

Flames sparked in her eyes. "You forbid me?"

I grinned and kissed her again. "Yes, I forbid you."

She punched me in the stomach. "The day I let you rule me, Nik Armstrong, is the day that I lose my mind." She punched me again. "As for making love twice a day… I've already done that this morning. I guess I'm free to do whatever else I please for the rest of the day."

I chuckled, rubbing the sore spot she had left on my abdomen. "Aww, man. I was hoping you would come upstairs with me and we could have some more fun."

"Maybe you should have said that before you *forbid* me." She gave me a deep smacking kiss then pushed off my lap. "Guess you will just have to wait." But she gave me a steamy look over her shoulder as she went into the house, a sly smile teasing her lips.

I grabbed the lyrics I had been working on for the new song, along with the sheet music I had been playing with, and chased after her.

Chapter 17

Just Another Day In The Demon's Lair

You would think that this is the part where I tell you time flies in the blink of an eye. But it didn't. Not really. At least not for me.

The next few months passed slowly, and I loved every minute of it. Well, mostly.

While we were still on the Gulf Coast, Emmie worked with a realtor via emails and online tours of some possible houses. By the time our vacation was over and we were making plans to head into the recording studio to work on some of the new material I had been slaving over, Emmie had found us a house—a huge six bedroom right on the beach in Malibu.

As big as the house was, Emmie needed help. I didn't want her to have to worry about the house, business issues, and the baby all at once. That was how Layla came into our lives. That little hottie not only tied my best friend in all kinds of knots, but she did the one thing I was sure was impossible. She became Emmie's best friend.

A miracle, right?

With Layla came two sisters that turned our lives upside down for entirely different reasons depending on whom you asked. Lucy captured my heart the first time I laid eyes on her. Sweet, imaginative, funny, and for me the little girl that Emmie should have gotten to be at that age. There wasn't one of us that wasn't caught in her spell, but that was okay. Lucy was special.

Then there was Lana. Beautiful. Feisty. Smarter than any one person had the right to be. Her biggest quality? She could make Drake laugh without even trying. My band brother was in deep within the first week of meeting Lana, and I wasn't sure if that was a good thing or not. That girl was just what he needed, but he fought it tooth and nail. Yet, at the same time he couldn't go two hours without talking to her.

Our strange little family of five—six, if you included Axton, which Emmie made sure that we did—grew by three. Other than Drake drinking more heavily, life was good for us. The only thing I really had to worry about was Emmie's C-section that the doctor said she had to have because the baby was too big for Emmie to have naturally.

The big day was creeping up on us fast. I had a week to finish up as much work in the studio as I possibly could before our baby girl joined us. So it was with complete reluctance that I climbed out of bed that morning and into the shower.

Downstairs Layla was already hard at work. It was hard for me not to hug her every time I saw her. Over the last few months she had taken such gentle care of Emmie, from taking her to the doctor when I wasn't able to, to consoling her when no one else could. And of course there was the baby shower that she had given Emmie, which had brought my girl to tears. I loved Layla for that alone.

"Don't let her overdo it," I told her with a smile as I grabbed a mug and poured a cup of Jesse's special blend of coffee.

Layla laughed, rolling her chocolate brown eyes at me. "Sure, I'll try."

The Rocker That Holds Her

I was rinsing my mug out when Jesse came into the kitchen with Drake and Shane. Jesse gave his girl a kiss goodbye and we were off to the studio for another day of recording. The morning went normally. Jesse was able to get the drums the exact way we wanted them on the second attempt, leaving me bewildered as always at how good he was. How could such a big man move so effortlessly when it came to playing the drums like that?

By lunch time I was starving, having skipped breakfast like I tended to do most mornings. Emmie's craving for bacon was starting to make even me hate the smell of frying pig in the morning.

Shane was in the middle of cracking jokes when Jesse's cell rang and then all hell broke loose.

Emmie's water had broken and Layla was rushing her to the hospital. Out of all the planning the doctor had prepared us for, he hadn't said anything about Emmie's water breaking or her going into labor. That was why he had scheduled the C-section at thirty-eight weeks, instead of waiting for her to go full term.

I was shaking as Jesse pushed me into the back seat of a taxi. My heart was racing and I was sure that I was having something close to a panic attack. I couldn't think about anything but Emmie and getting to her. She must be terrified.

When the doctor had first told her that she had to have the C-section she had lost it. Her fear alone had scared me. Layla had helped, and then the doctor had made sure that the rest of the guys and I knew exactly what was going to happen. I had been ready, at least that was what I had been telling myself about ten times a day for the last few weeks.

I wasn't fucking ready. I was never going to be ready! Emmie was going to have major surgery, and even I knew that there could be any kind of unforeseen complication. My stomach twisted and turned and I was close to vomiting by the time the taxi reached the Women's Center. The car hadn't even completely stopped and I was opening the door, needing to get to Emmie now.

I saw a desk and stopped for directions, knowing that I couldn't find her without help. But when I opened my mouth to talk, I started babbling like a stroke victim. Jesse saved my ass and asked the questions that I couldn't.

The elevator ride was nerve-racking. I was sure I could have ran up the stairs faster than that damned thing moved. When we stepped off a nurse's station stood in our way. Again, it was Jesse who did the talking. The lie that we had been telling everyone since the day Emmie's mother died slipped from his lips and then someone was pointing the way to where I wanted to be the most.

I ran like my life depended on it, and in this case it did. Emmie was the only thing in the world that mattered. When I skidded to a halt in her room it was to find nurses and a doctor that I had never seen before rushing around, talking so fast that it made my head spin. My eyes went to Emmie and my heart actually stopped.

She looked so small in that big hospital bed—pale with tears running down her face. For the first time since Layla's frantic phone call, I felt tears starting to burn my own eyes and I rushed toward her. Her arms were trembling as she wrapped them around my neck and I buried my face in her neck.

"Are you okay?" I whispered.

"I hurt," she told me in a shaky voice that wasn't like my Emmie at all. "The contractions are coming faster."

I gulped in a few deep breaths. I wanted to just lose it right then. Emmie was the strong one, not me. But I knew that this time I had to be her strength. I mentally started praying to every one of those damned gods that Emmie swore by. I begged for the safe delivery of my baby girl, for them to watch over and protect Em, and for the ability to help Emmie through this like I needed to. While I prayed mentally, I talked to Emmie trying to keep her calm. She was shaking badly and I wasn't sure if it was because she was so scared, in so much pain, or a mixture of both.

Things were moving faster than I could possibly imagine and before I knew it a nurse was pushing me toward the bathroom with a pair of scrubs. I left Emmie with the guys, knowing that they would protect her with their lives in the few minutes it would take me to change.

I had to wait outside the operating room while they gave Emmie her epidural. It took them ten minutes to do that, and it was the longest ten minutes of my life. When they finally let me in, Em was lying flat on her back. A tent separated her head from the rest of her body so she couldn't see what was going on with the doctor and his team.

I tried not to think about what the doctor was doing to Emmie as I took the seat the nurse said was for me. Tears were pouring down Emmie's face when I sat down beside her and took her trembling hand. "Are you in pain?"

She shook her head. "No... Just scared."

I gave her the best smile I could muster. "Me too," I admitted.

"It's been a roller coaster the last five months, hasn't it?" she whispered.

"Roller coasters are fun," I assured her, leaning closer so I could kiss away her tears. The sight of her damp face hurt me like nothing else could, and I wanted to take all the pain and anxiety away for her.

"Okay, Emmie. It won't be long now. Another minute and this baby will be all yours." The doctor spoke up from the other side of the tent. "How you doing?"

"There's a lot of pressure," she told him.

"That's normal considering I'm pushing around inside of you." The doctor paused and then he was talking to the team of nurses and other medical staff around him. Asking for suction, demanding a clamp here and one there. I was terrified with each new command that left his mouth.

The room grew completely quiet as he started tugging and pulling and Emmie cried out, her hand tightening around my own to the point that I was sure I was going to have a few crushed bones in my hand. "Emmie?" I stroked her hair with my free hand. "Talk to me, baby."

"I… I'm okay," she whispered.

"Here she is!" the doctor announced, and then the room was filled with a sound I had never thought was pleasant but suddenly sounded like the most beautiful thing I had ever heard.

My daughter started to cry, making her presence known in the world.

Tears burned my eyes and I was unable to contain them this time as a nurse urged me to follow her and the screaming bundle in her arms. I watched them intently as they wiped some smelly goo off my child. She was weighed and measured. A little cloth cap was put on her head, and she was wrapped in a clean blanket.

And then I was being handed the most precious little bundle in the world. She didn't smell good at all, and she was a squealing, angry mess. But the instant she was placed in my arms, my heart filled with the kind of love I knew I had never felt before.

For months I had thought I knew what it was like to love the child I knew was growing inside of Emmie. But now that I actually had her in my arms, I was aware that those feelings had only been for a dream. Reality was so much stronger, so much better.

I hugged her close, talking softly to the still crying baby. But the more I talked, the calmer she became until she was completely quiet, seeming to hang onto my every word as I told her how happy I was to finally meet her.

"Nik?"

Emmie's weak voice reached me and I rushed back to her, still holding onto the baby. The doctors were working fast to get Emmie put back together, and she looked exhausted when I sat down on the chair beside of her. "Look at what I have, Em." I smiled through my tears and positioned the baby so Emmie could see our daughter. "She's so beautiful, baby."

"Is she okay?"

"She's perfect," I assured her.

A nurse came up beside me telling Emmie all about height and weight and something about an Apgar score. Whatever Apgar happened to be, the baby's seemed to be good, and Emmie was smiling as she started to drift off to sleep.

Chapter 18

Once Upon A Time

Mia Nicole Armstrong came home later than we had originally expected, and so did Emmie.

Mia had jaundice, and not just a little bit either. She looked like an Umpa Lumpa from *Willy Wonka and The Chocolate Factory* by the second day. Her pediatrician said that it was because Emmie's blood type was so different from my own and that Mia had my blood type. She had to be put under a light that would help bring her bilirubin levels down. During that time I felt such heartache and panic that it made my chest hurt to the point that I was sure I was having an anxiety attack.

The doctor and nurses kept trying to reassure us all that Mia was going to be okay. Jaundice was completely common when it came to newborns. I had to keep reminding myself that Mia was okay, that there were babies that were sicker and not nearly as lucky. If the nurses thought that I was an over anxious daddy, it was nothing compared to Emmie.

She was a wreck. The minute they put the little blindfold on Mia and put her under the light Emmie became hysterical. She tore her stitches from the C-section and had to be sedated for two days to keep her in bed.

It was a scary week and I was beyond happy to get home with my family.

Of course that all flew out the window when Emmie's postpartum depression set in. My Gods! Were all women like that after having a baby? She could flay me alive with just a look, and her tongue was so sharp it left me bleeding from the inside out. And when she wasn't tearing me and the others apart, she was crying.

Emmie's scars from her mother went deeper than any of us could possibly have guessed. She was terrified of being a bad mother. Em wanted to take care of Mia herself. All of my help was shunned. I couldn't pick Mia up when she was crying without causing an argument, something I tried to avoid. Everything was adding up and Emmie was looking worse and worse every day.

I spent more and more time in the studio so I wasn't in Emmie's way. It was killing me that I couldn't help her or comfort her. Staying away was the only thing I could think of to ease some of her stress.

One evening Layla met me at the door as soon as I got home with the guys. She had the baby in her arms and the baby monitor in one hand. I frowned at the combination. Shouldn't the monitor have only been necessary if the baby was in her crib?

"What's up?" I asked, staring down at Mia with a tired smile. Just because Emmie wasn't letting me help didn't mean that I was getting any sleep when she got up with Mia throughout the night.

"Emmie has been sleeping all day," Layla told me quietly. "I think she's going to calm down and let you start helping her more."

I felt tears stinging my eyes and blinked them a few times to keep from embarrassing myself in front of Layla. "Is she okay?"

Layla gave me a small smile, her chocolate eyes full of understanding. "She's fine. Just exhausted." She carefully placed Mia in my arms before turning to put the monitor on a table. "I've been listening for Emmie. She's probably starving. I made dinner so you can just reheat it when she's ready."

I glanced from Layla to Mia, who was safely bundled up in my arms. She was frowning up at me, and I suspected that she was making a mess in her diaper. "Thanks for helping, Layla," I told the woman that had become such a lifeline in my life lately. Emmie didn't listen to anyone but Layla right now.

"No thanks needed." She pushed her long cinnamon hair out of her face and gave me a smile. "If you need anything, just call or come over."

After Layla had gone home, I carried Mia upstairs and took care of the diaper issue. I had only changed about five diapers since she had been born, and never one so messy. But I muddled through, talking quietly to the baby as I cleaned her up and put a new sleeper on her. Mia was only a few weeks old, but she listened to my voice so intently that it seemed like she understood every word that I said.

Exhausted from having only gotten a little over an hour sleep the night before, I dropped down in the rocking chair beside Mia's crib in the nursery and cuddled my baby close. "Mommy has been bonkers lately, huh, Mia?" I grinned down at her when she frowned at me yet again, not to fill her diaper but as if she didn't like me talking about her mother like that. "But we still love her, don't we?"

The baby's only reply was to blow a bubble at me. "Daddy's going to make sure that Mommy doesn't get like that again." I realized that I hadn't been acting much like a daddy lately. Instead of staying away in hopes that Emmie would just get better on her own, I should have been insisting on helping her. I felt like I had let both Em and Mia down.

Determined to make it up to two of the most important people in my world, I brushed a kiss over Mia's forehead. "How about a story, baby doll?" I crossed my legs and put the baby carefully on my lap, stroking my fingers over her face and peach fuzz hair that I knew was going to be just like her mothers. "Once upon a time there was a beautiful little girl with a tear streaked face. She had no idea that the boy next door was going to spend the rest of his life loving her…"

--

A cool hand brushed over my cheek and my eyes snapped open. Big green eyes set in a thin, pale face filled my vision. There were dark circles under Emmie's eyes, so bad that it looked like bruises. Memories of her actually having a black eye from one of her mother's rages filled my mind, and I reached out a hand to grasp her.

She gave me a small smile and sat down on the edge of the rocking chair. "Hi," Emmie murmured before turning her gaze to the sleeping baby lying across my chest on her stomach.

"How are you feeling?" I whispered, trying not to wake the baby. I hadn't remembered falling asleep, but it must have been a while ago. My neck was stiff and my body was protesting from sitting too long.

Emmie sighed. "Better. I slept eighteen hours."

"This is my fault. I should have made you let me help out with the baby. Instead, I took the easy way out and let you deal with it all."

Emmie rolled her eyes. "Since when can you *make* me do anything, Nik?"

I wrapped my free arm around Emmie's tiny waist. She had lost the pregnancy belly and had lost more weight than I wanted to think about since Mia had been born. Gods, I sucked at taking care of my girls. "Yeah, but I need to start."

"If you say so." She leaned against me, putting her head on my chest much like Mia was. "This is my fault, Nik. No one's but my own. I was jealous. Mia loves you so much, and she does nothing but cry when I hold her."

I sighed. "Ah, Em, she can sense your stress. That's why she cries so much when you hold her. You have been so tired, so anxious. Mia can feel all of that. Fuck, baby. We all could." I combed my fingers through her hair, trying to soothe her as I had done to Mia earlier. "If you would just relax everything will be okay."

"I want to be a good mom…" Emmie whispered with a small hitch in her voice that told me she was close to tears.

"You are a great mom. The best mom. Mia is so lucky to have you, baby."

How could I relieve her fears? How did I make her understand that she was never going to be the mom her own mother had been? I wasn't sure that I, or anyone else, ever could. If she didn't get things just right in her own estimations on how a mother was supposed to be, Emmie thought she was a bad mother. It was going to drive her—and everyone around her—insane.

"Listen to me, Em. Worrying about being a good mother, about getting it right… That alone is the sign of a great mom. You love Mia and you want what is best for her. Fuck, Em. You have put her well-being before your own already. In my book you already qualify as mother of the year."

She gave a soft, quiet little laugh, and I brushed a kiss over the top of her head. "You had the worst mother in the world, Em. I hate that and her. But you know what *not* to do because of her."

"What if I mess up?"

"Then you learn from it and move on. But guess what?"

She raised her head. "What?"

"We can mess it up together. Mia has us both." I glanced from Emmie to the only other person in the world that could stop my heart from beating by just looking at her. "I want to be a good daddy just as much as you want to be a good mom. I didn't have much of a role model either."

"Are you as scared as I am?"

"Probably more."

"She's going to have more than we did."

I chuckled softly. "Of course she is. She's a rock princess after all. Mia is going to own the world."

A giggle escaped Emmie and the sound went straight through my heart and down to my dick. It had been months since I had made love to Em. The last trimester of pregnancy had been too uncomfortable for Emmie to have sex. We hadn't done more than heavy petting for so long, and my body felt like it was on constant alert for any signs of attention. It hadn't mattered to me that we hadn't made love. I wasn't going to do anything to hurt Emmie.

That didn't mean I didn't ache for her though…

"I meant love, stupid," she corrected me. "Yeah. Mia will have plenty of that," I assured her with a tender kiss on her lips.

Chapter 19

No, Is So Heart Shattering

Thanksgiving was fast approaching and I was getting a little anxious. When I had asked Emmie to marry me, she had said yes, but only after the baby was born.

Well, now Mia was here and Emmie hadn't even mentioned getting married. I was so ready to make everything legit. I wanted Emmie as my wife, not just my *baby momma* as the tabloids described her recently when they had run the story of Mia's birth.

I was worried that Emmie thought I wasn't serious about getting married. We hadn't discussed it since I had asked her all those months ago. Maybe she thought I had only asked to prove a point, not because I really wanted to. The truth was I wanted it more than anything I had ever wanted before.

Okay, I'll admit that when I first started accepting my feelings for Emmie for what they really were I had been scared out of my mind. Marriage had terrified me back then. In the world of rock 'n' roll, of any celebrity really, marriages didn't last long. The touring, the crazy fans, the whole fucking lifestyle was rough on a relationship. But hell, Emmie had put up with me and that lifestyle for longer than most marriages lasted. I had faith that we could make it work now.

To show her how serious I was about marrying her I went shopping. It took me two days to find the ring I wanted. A five carat princess cut engagement ring that was handcrafted by one of the most sought after jewelry designers on the planet. It cost an ugly amount of money, which was nearly impossible to keep from Emmie until I gave it to her.

Luckily I had Axton. With Jesse and Drake distracted by their own relationships, and Shane doing only gods knew what, Axton was the only other friend I really had that I could ask for help. To keep Emmie from finding out before I wanted her to, I asked Axton to buy the ring and I would pay him back once Emmie had the ring.

Axton handed over his credit card without a blink of an eye. "Treat her right, man," he advised me with a sad smile.

I clasped my friend's hand in a tight handshake. "Always."

With the ring in hand I set out to make this proposal at least a little more romantic than the last one I had made. Layla agreed to babysit Mia for us while I took Emmie out for the first time since the baby had been born.

I had never been so nervous in my life, and I wasn't even sure why. She had already agreed to marry me. I had my yes. Now I just needed to give her the ring and ask her to set a date. The sooner the better.

A limo was already waiting on us as we stepped outside and I helped Emmie into the back seat. She gave me a grin as she scooted over, and I climbed in beside her. "This is unexpected."

"I thought I would spoil you just a little."

She reached for my hand, linking our fingers. "Thanks, Nik."

I pulled her against me. "I love you, Em."

"Still?" She grinned, but I saw the uncertainty in the green depths of her eyes. It gutted me to see it. "I figured that after the last few weeks I had driven all that love away."

Her postpartum depression hadn't completely disappeared overnight. She was still struggling with it, but I hadn't let her push me away again. She had my complete support now. "No, baby. Nothing you do will ever stop me from loving you."

I held her close as the driver managed to get us to our destination. We had dinner at one of LA's most popular restaurants. I had thought about giving her the ring after dinner, but knew she would think it was too cheesy.

She was laughing and clinging to my side as we got back into the limo, more relaxed than I had seen her in weeks. I pulled her legs across my lap and held onto her left hand as the driver pulled into traffic. "Did you enjoy tonight?"

"It was the best." She leaned back in the corner of the seat, her head resting on the door. "Thanks, babe."

"It's not over." I reached into my pocket for the little box I had been carrying for two days now. I had been so worried about her finding the ring that I had kept it with me since I bought it.

Her head jerked up when she saw the box and she reached for the button to turn the lights on overhead. "What is this?" she demanded.

My anxiety returned and I tightened my hold on her hand when she started to pull away. Opening the box, I took the ring and slipped it onto her finger. Her eyes widened. "Are you crazy?"

"About you, yes." I laughed, trying to hide my fears.

"That's an engagement ring…" she suddenly whispered, going from demanding to dazed in the blink of an eye.

"Of course it is. Engaged women normally wear them."

"But…" She frowned, breaking off and staring down at the ring that fit perfectly on her finger.

"You said that once Mia was born we would get married. You haven't even mentioned it." I didn't confess that I was scared out of my mind that she wasn't going to marry me after all. That she didn't want to marry me… "I realized that maybe since I hadn't given you a ring you thought that I hadn't been serious when I asked you."

She swallowed hard, her face looking paler than I had seen it in weeks. "No, I knew you were serious."

"When do you want to get married? I was thinking next month." Christmas was a good a time as any to get married, right?

"No." She shook her head, some of the dazed look fading from her eyes.

"Okay, how about January? That is plenty of time for you to find a dress."

"I don't want to get married in January either…" She tugged her hand free, and I reluctantly let her go. "I… I'm not sure I want to get married at all."

All the color drained from my face as all my fears rushed to the surface. She didn't want to marry me? No, no, no. She couldn't possibly have said that. I wasn't hearing her right. "What?" I croaked out.

Green eyes darkened to a shade I had rarely seen. "I love you, Nik. More than anything. But... why do we have to get married? We're happy. You, Mia, and me are a family. That's enough for me."

My fingers actually trembled as I raked them through my hair. "Well it isn't enough for me!" The words came out harsher than I wanted them, but I was suddenly hurting in a way I had never hurt before. Emmie didn't want to marry me. She didn't love me enough to become my wife.

My world felt like it was crashing around me.

This wasn't happening. It couldn't be happening. I had everything I wanted, except Emmie as my wife. When she had said yes to marrying me all those months ago, I had accepted that as proof of how much she loved me. Just as she had trust issues, so did I. And now my trust was starting to crumble.

Maybe Emmie didn't love me as much as I thought.

--

It took me four days to come to my senses. Four days of pain that went soul deep and left me feeling as if I had a mortal wound that kept festering every time I so much as looked at Emmie. We had been fighting almost constantly over the last four days. Not over getting married, because she refused to talk about *that*. But everything else, even the way I burped Mia, was a subject that had us practically screaming at each other.

The Rocker That Holds Her

On the fifth day, I woke up to an empty bed and realized I was out of my mind. Emmie was just scared. That was the only reason I could come up with to explain her refusal to get married. She hated change. Change had always been a bad thing in her eyes.

The first change I had forced on her was when I had left with the band. Her life had been turned upside down with no one around to take care of her while she had to deal with her mother. The second was when we brought her to live with us on the road. While that hadn't been traumatic, it had been life changing and probably scary for the fifteen year old she had been. And then when Mia had come she had been so sick with her postpartum depression that she had nearly lost herself for a while.

Her fear of change had kept her from admitting her feelings for me. That fear had her begging Shane, Drake, and Jesse not to leave her when we had finally settled down in Malibu. And now I could see that that same fear was keeping her from marrying me.

I had to give her time and pray that she would realize that out of all the changes I had made in her life, marrying me was not going to hurt her in any way.

It was with that mentality that I stepped into the shower. Fifteen minutes later I was downstairs following my nose to something that smelled so good my stomach growled in appreciation. Steak and eggs! Oh sweet heavens.

The kitchen was busy this morning. Layla was cooking for everyone while Jesse had a goofy grin on his face. Shane was at the kitchen table with Lana and Drake talking about plans for the night while Emmie spoke rapidly on her phone with a determined look on her face that told me she was taking care of some business issue.

"Morning people," I greeted, noticing that Lucy and Mia were absent from our family gathering. "Where are the babies?"

"Morning." Layla gave me a megawatt smile that had me stumbling a little at how beautiful it was. Shit, she was pretty when she was happy. "Lucy is still at her sleepover and should be home soon. Mia is napping."

I stopped pulling out the chair between Emmie and Lana. "Okay, what did I miss?"

Jesse grabbed hold of Layla's waist and pulled her down onto his lap. "Congratulate me, bro. I'm getting married today."

For one brief second I was overcome with jealousy. Jesse had known his girl all of five minutes and he was already getting married. Meanwhile, Emmie had always been my other half and I couldn't get her to even talk about the dreaded M-word. It wasn't fair any way I looked at it.

But then my love for my band brother and best friend pushed down that evil jealous monster, and I was thrilled for the happy couple. I vetoed the chair and went around the table to clap the big bald rocker on the back. "That's fucking awesome, Jess! Congrats, dude." I bent my head and brushed a quick kiss over Layla's cheek. "Welcome to the family, Lay."

Emmie tossed her iPhone onto the table, a grin on her face. "It's set. I got the nicest chapel in Vegas and was able to get us all rooms for tonight at the hotel we normally stay in. As soon as Lucy gets home we can go."

The Rocker That Holds Her

Jesse let out a *whoop* and kissed Layla long and hard. I dropped down in my seat beside Emmie and reached for the plate of breakfast that Layla had made for me. Shane and Drake were talking about their own plans for after the wedding while Lana looked almost hung over. I shot her a concerned glance, noticing her pale face and set jaw. Drake asked her a question and she gave a tight smile and remained silent.

I worried about her as I ate my breakfast, but before I could question her, she excused herself to pack for the overnight trip. I grimaced as I watched her walk away. Whatever was wrong with her I didn't feel like I had a right to ask questions, but if she didn't look better by the time we left for Vegas I would ask Jesse to talk to her.

After I rinsed my plate and put it in the dishwasher—something I had come a little more accustomed to doing since we had first moved in—I headed upstairs to pack. Emmie had enough to worry about with getting Mia ready to go to have to deal with packing my things. To my surprise, however, she was sitting on our bed when I walked into the bedroom.

I raised an eyebrow at her as I crossed over to my closet and pulled my smaller suitcase from the back. "I figured you would be running around getting Mia's things set."

"I did that already." She stood and I sensed her walking toward me. "Can we talk?"

I shot her a glance over my shoulder. "Yeah, sure, baby."

I grabbed a pair of jeans and tossed them in the open case then turned to face her. As she walked toward me I noticed the ring I had given her winking back at me. I took it as a good sign that despite the fact Emmie refused to get married, she hadn't taken her engagement ring off once—not even when she slept. Emmie didn't even sleep with her nose ring in, so why the engagement ring?

Emmie bit her lip and I had to look away. Dammit, I wanted her so bad I was one big ache. We hadn't had sex in months, and for the last five days we hadn't so much as kissed or held each other at night. "We've been arguing a lot and I hate it. I know that I made you mad the other night when I told you I don't want to get married. I'm sorry, Nik."

Despite my throbbing body and the fear that I would come in my pants at just a brush of her body against mine, I reached out and pulled her against me. I couldn't stand the distance that I had inadvertently caused between us. I had been so anxious to get her to set a date that I had nearly ruined everything between us. "I'm sorry, Emmie. I shouldn't have pushed so hard. You still have fears, and I will try my damnedest not to rush you. I just hope that one day what we have will seem too little and you will want more with me."

Her eyes darkened with something I couldn't decipher. I didn't question it as I brushed a tender kiss over her lips and stepped back before I embarrassed myself by spraying in my shorts at even that innocent contact.

Chapter 20

...Emmie...

It was a bitch trying to put a wedding together in less than twenty-four hours.

I was on my phone nearly the entire way to Vegas. Just because I had the chapel ready to go and hotel rooms reserved for everyone didn't mean that everything was ready. I had to make sure that all the guys got tuxes. No way was I going to let my best girlfriend get married with her man in jeans and a Demon's Wings T-shirt.

Plus there was a wedding dress and bridesmaid dresses for the rest of us to buy, not to mention flowers and a bouquet for Layla. At one point I had to reach back into the back seat of the Escalade and pull Layla off of Jesse to find out what flowers she liked more. I was more amused than annoyed. Jesse hadn't let Layla get more than a few inches away from him all morning. Poor Layla was going to be brain dead before the wedding even took place because he was depriving her of oxygen the way he continued to kiss her.

I watched Lucy as she gave her sister and soon-to-be brother-in-law a disgusted grimace. She was still a little dazed from all the excitement. After getting home from her first sleepover she had been rushed into the third row of the Escalade and told Layla was getting married. She seemed both happy and frightened at the same time. I couldn't blame her. In her young life she had been tossed upside down more than her fair share—the death of her mother, moving in with a sister she didn't know, then moving next door to a bunch of rowdy rock stars. Now her world was changing even more with the addition of a brother-in-law and another move—even if the move was a mere two houses down.

I felt her fears because I had been having some of my own for the last five days. Why couldn't Nik be happy with the way things were? Most men in the world would be ecstatic if their girlfriend told them that they didn't want marriage.

But Nik did. He wanted it more than I have ever known him to want anything.

Marriage wasn't something I was ready for. At least that was what I kept telling myself. Besides, I knew that I was going to love Nik for the rest of my life. Just as I knew that given the chance I would have at least one more child with him. Marriage on the other hand…it kind of terrified me in a way nothing else had. Even motherhood didn't scare me as bad as the thought of marriage did.

Maybe it was because marriage meant that things were going to change again. I wasn't good with change. It had rarely been a good thing for me. Moving to Ohio from West Virginia at the age of five had been good in that I had met the guys. But that all changed when the band had signed on with Rich as their manager and a record label had picked them up. The years without them had been bleak to say the least. When I had found out I was pregnant, I worried that I would lose Jesse, Drake, and Shane—three of the most important people in my life. I hadn't been able to face a reality where they weren't right down the hall on a daily basis.

Having Mia had brought a change that had been all on me. I had changed to the point that for a few weeks I didn't even recognize myself. I was still struggling a little with it, but it wasn't nearly as bad as it had been.

Yet even having lost myself couldn't compare to the fear of losing what I could possibly lose if I got married—Nik. I was sure that I would lose Nik if I married him. That fear was so acute, so fucking strong that I could taste my fear when I let myself think about it. I could face letting Jesse, Drake, and Shane living their own lives. I could handle losing myself in the fog of postpartum depression.

But I wouldn't survive if I lost Nik…

Nik pulled to a stop in front of the hotel, and I rushed everyone through check-in. The next few hours were crazy, busy, and I will admit a little fun. Between Layla, Lana, and even Lucy I was hard pressed not to find something to laugh about.

It wasn't until we were in the chapel with Layla and Jesse exchanging their vows that my mind started racing. Something Nik had said before we had left the house kept nagging at me. *I just hope that one day what we have will seem too little and you will want more with me.* Was that what he really thought?

The more I thought about it the faster my heart raced. I watched Layla and Jesse, tears in their eyes as they pledged to love each other for the rest of their lives. Hadn't I already done that with Nik in my heart? Wasn't I his wife in my soul already?

I glanced down at the ring that sat so perfectly on my left hand. I hadn't been able to take it off, not even at night. I couldn't stand to sleep in jewelry and felt tangled and restrained even when wearing earrings. So why hadn't I taken off the ring?

Because under all the fear, I *wanted* to marry Nik.

I nearly laughed out loud at how stupid I had been acting. Marrying Nik wouldn't cause me to lose him, but not marrying him might!

A new fear twisted in my stomach. What if Nik decided that my not wanting to marry him meant I didn't love him? That to me our relationship wasn't important enough to me to take it to the next level?

Jesse and Layla were halfway down the aisle, their hands already all over each other as they walked, before I snapped out of my stupor. Nik was standing there, his hand out to me so I could walk down the aisle with him after our friends. Tears filled my eyes and I threw myself into his waiting arms.

"I'm sorry!" I pushed back enough to look up at him, hoping that he could see how much I loved him shining through my eyes. "I'm so sorry, Nik. I love you. I want to get married."

Behind me Jesse joked and I only half listened. My attention was focused on Nik, watching as his eyes filled with tears and a smile lifted his kissable lips. "Will you marry me, Nik?"

He laughed and it was then that I realized that I would never have to fear losing Nik. "Yes, Emmie. I'll marry you."

--

Mia was sound sleep when I got out of the shower. Nik was relaxed on the bed with the remote in one hand flipping through the channels, looking for the scores of the college football games he had missed today. While he was distracted, I took my time looking at the man that was going to be my husband in a little over a year; we had already set the date.

Having showered after I put Mia down for the night in the crib provided by the hotel, Nik had only bothered with putting a pair of boxers on. His free hand was lying on his stomach and his blue eyes were half-closed in relaxation. I was hoping to *un*-relax him in the next few minutes.

"How did the Buckeyes fare today?" I asked, untying the gray silk robe I had picked up while shopping for Layla's wedding dress earlier.

"Haven't seen their scores yet." Nik tossed the remote aside, bored with the television, before finally raising his eyes to me.

When that blue gaze landed on my red teddy, his eyes dilated with passion and I watched as his boxers suddenly became a tent from the erection he instantly got. My nipples tightened in response to his instant reaction to me. It had been so long since I felt his hands on me, and I was aching for them right now.

"Wh-what's this?" he asked in a voice so gravely with desire it sounded almost animalistic.

"I saw the doctor yesterday," I told him. The appointment had gone well, and I had even decided to start taking the pill so Nik wouldn't have to worry about condoms. "As long as we don't get carried away, it's okay to have sex again."

The words hadn't fully left my mouth before he was grabbing me and pulling me onto the bed. Nik moved fast, covering me with his big, hard body and slamming his mouth down on mine. When he finally pulled back we were both gasping for breath.

"I'll be careful, baby. I swear I won't hurt you."

My fingers were trembling with both passion and love as I lifted them to trace his damp mouth. "I know, Nik. I love you."

His eyes darkened even more. "I love you too, Em." Warm lips brushed over mine in a butterfly caress before kissing across my cheek, down my neck, and pausing to nuzzle my ear. "I know that getting married is a big deal for you. Thank you for making every dream I have ever had come true."

Tears burned the backs of my eyes, and I blinked rapidly to keep them at bay. I had cried far too much in recent weeks. I didn't want to cry when I was so happy. "I was terrified that I would lose you if we got married," I confessed my unnatural fear.

He pulled back enough to meet my gaze. "That is the stupidest thing I have ever heard." He shook his head sadly. "You're stuck with me no matter what, Em. It nearly destroyed me when you said you didn't want to marry me, but I still couldn't walk away from you."

One errant tear spilled down my cheek, and I dashed it away with the back of my hand. "I'm sorry I hurt you," I whispered. It gutted me to know that I had caused him pain like that.

His long fingered hand cupped my left breast, his thumb brushing over my distended nipple. That one touch and I felt like I was on fire with need. I wanted him so bad that I was sure I would come at the first touch of his fingers on my pussy. My thighs spread as if they had a will of their own, and Nik came down over me, his pulsing dick pressed against me perfectly.

"Fuck, you feel so damn good!" he muttered, his jaw clenched as if he were having just as much trouble holding on to his self-control as I was. "This is going to be over embarrassingly fast, baby." He buried his face in my neck while his hands were busy touching me everywhere. "I'm so close I don't think I can last much longer."

He moved his hips just a little and his dick brushed over my clit. Even through the thin layers of clothing that still separated us that one small contact had me panting. I clutched at his bare back, my nails sinking into his skin so hard that they nearly broke through. I let out a small scream only to bite my lip, scared I would wake Mia who was across the room in her crib.

"Looks like I'm not the only one," he rasped out, gritting his teeth so hard I could hear it even through the blood rushing through my ears. "Gods, I love it when you're wild like this."

I arched my back, pressing my pussy against his dick harder. "Fuck me, now," I commanded. "Or I'm going to attack your sexy ass."

Fingers that trembled unsnapped my teddy at the crotch. Seconds later, Nik was pushing inside of me. It had been so long, and I was tighter than I had ever been. If I hadn't wanted him so desperately, if I wasn't soaking wet for him, it would have hurt.

Nik thrust halfway in and stopped. He was holding on to his control by a ragged thread, and the effort was costing him dearly. His entire face was clenched, veins popping up in his neck and forehead as he gasped for breath. "Am I…hurting…you?" he gritted out.

He was harder than I could remember him being. His dick pulsed inside of me, and I shuddered with pleasure. "I'm good. I'm better…than good." Sweat dripped down Nik's face and my entire body was damp with my own perspiration. Less than five minutes and I was in need of another shower. "Please, move."

"You're so tight, baby." He shifted his hips just a little, gaining half an inch deeper. "Don't want to hurt you."

My need for him was flooding my pussy more and more with each passing second. There was no way he could hurt me. Not when it felt this fucking amazing. "You won't. I swear. Please, Nik. I want you so bad."

He groaned and pulled almost completely out of me. I whimpered in protest, wanting him deep. "Nik! I'll beg if you want me to."

Nik muttered a harsh curse and slammed back into me, going balls deep. There was nothing that could possibly compare to how good he felt deep inside of me like that. I clung to him as he slowly pulled out of me only to dive deep again. I was shaking, so close to the edge of my release that I wasn't sure I was going to survive the fall.

"Emmie, I love you!" Nik whispered, thrusting deep one final time.

His words sent me over the edge. Those sweet words that I had never thought I would hear him say pushed me to a release that left me free falling. I cried out, not sure what exactly I was saying, as I felt him coming apart in my arms.

<u>Epilogue</u>

Wedding Day

I woke up in an empty bed.

Groaning, I turned over on the king sized mattress, burying my face in the pillows and wishing that Emmie was beside me. My body ached with need for her, having spent the last two days without her. Layla, Lana, and Harper had taken Emmie to some spa for the last two days. Their version of a bachelorette party.

I was glad that Emmie was off having fun, being spoiled rotten and pampered as she got ready for our wedding. My aching dick on the other hand wanted to strangle all three of the females that had become vital parts of our family.

"Da-da!"

I raised my head, my body instantly cooling down at the sound of Mia. My partially closed bedroom door opened and in toddled my baby girl. Emmie was going to freak when she found out that Mia could climb out of her crib now, something that she had been doing for the last two days.

Sixteen month old Mia pushed her tousled red hair back from her baby doll face. Big, sleepy green eyes spotted me as I sat up in bed. "Da-da!" she exclaimed, running toward me as fast as her chubby little legs could carry her while she held on tightly to the little bear in her arms. As soon as she reached my side of the bed, I swung her up into my arms.

She clung happily to my neck. "Da-da..." She pulled back, noticing that the spot beside me was empty yet again. Her bottom lip trembled. "Mo-ma?"

I gave her a reassuring smile. "Momma will be home today, baby doll." I brushed a kiss over her sweet smelling hair. "And you get to wear your pretty flower fairy dress."

Mia didn't seem to care that she was going to get to dress up in the beautiful dress that Emmie and Layla had picked out for her last month. She looked up at me with a pout before climbing down from my lap and snuggling into her mother's pillows. "Mo-ma."

I rolled my eyes. Yeah, she was too much like her mother. And whether Emmie realized it or not, Mia was just as much a momma's girl as she was a daddy's girl. I jumped out of bed, anxious to start the day. By tonight Emmie would be my wife, and I was finding it hard to contain my nervous excitement.

Downstairs I found Jesse, Shane, and Drake already sitting at the kitchen table. There was a pot of Jesse's special recipe coffee sitting in the middle while my three band brothers sat quietly.

"What's up?" I questioned, going to the cabinet to grab a mug along with a box of Cheerios and a bowl for Mia, who was already climbing onto Drake's lap.

"Just remembering the old days," Jesse muttered, frowning down into his mug. His jaw was clenched and he kept averting his eyes.

"It seems like yesterday that Emmie was just a dirty little rag doll that we tried to take care of..." Shane sighed, a sound that sounded a little sad.

Drake arranged Mia on his lap so she could eat her breakfast and still hug him. I let my eyes linger on my daughter, suddenly understanding what was wrong with my friends. It was going to be hard for me when it came time for Mia to get married. I was already dreading the day when I had to hand my baby doll over to some nameless asshole.

For the guys—but especially for Jesse—that was what they were doing today. They loved Emmie in an entirely different way than I did. For them she was their sister, and in some ways their daughter. Jesse had always been the one that came the closest to being the only father figure that Em ever had. Today he was handing his little girl over into my safe keeping, even if she had already been there for years.

I reached over and clasped his shoulder. "I'll take good care of her, man."

Jesse clenched his jaw, looked away, and nodded his bald head. "Yeah…" he cleared his throat "…yeah, man. I know you will."

An hour later people started showing up. The caterers started setting up in the kitchen while outside a tent was being set up on the beach. February was the wettest month in Malibu, and Emmie hadn't wanted to chance being rained on. But she hadn't needed to worry. The sun was shining brightly and the temperature continued to rise higher than normal.

I kept Mia inside. The guys and I played with her non stop trying to pass the hours away until it was time to start getting ready. The wedding wasn't until six and the girls weren't going to arrive until three. By that time I was expected to be in the guest house with the guys, keeping away from Emmie until she walked down the aisle.

At two thirty I ushered Mia outside and into the guesthouse. Four tuxes were already hanging up in the bedroom along with Mia's dress. As the time slowly ticked down, I found myself taking on the characteristics of my band brothers. I started pacing, trying to burn off some of the anxiety. My fingers tugged at my hair as I alternated between fear of Emmie deciding that she didn't want to get married after all and calm because I knew Emmie would never do that to me.

At three thirty Lucy walked into the guesthouse. She looked adorable in her silvery dress with flowers and little jewels braided into her dark hair. Lucy handed Jesse a folded piece of paper. "Dad, you aren't answering your phone. Aunt Em said to give this to you."

Jesse frowned and reached for his cellphone in his back pocket. "It's dead." Taking the paper his ever changing dark eyes narrowed and he crumbled the paper in his hands. "Okay. Tell Em I'll take care of it."

Lucy only nodded and rushed off to relay the message. My heart was beating me to death in my chest. "What?" I demanded. "What's wrong?"

Jesse shook his head. "It's nothing, man. Just a little disagreement with Rich. I'll deal with it."

I muttered a curse. We had fired Rich as our manager the second week of January. Our contract had expired on New Year's Day and Rich hadn't seemed to wonder why we hadn't signed a new one. When he had realized that we weren't going to, he had gone ballistic. OtherWorld had dropped Rich the year before, and now with Demon's Wings doing the same thing, Rich was going to lose clients left and right. Rumors were already flying that he might have to file bankruptcy by the end of the year if any other big names fired him.

We hadn't found a new manger to replace Rich because Demon's Wings had always had one. Emmie had taken care of us practically from the day she moved in with us. After all those years of learning the ropes she had the know-how as well as the connections to make sure that Demon's Wings stayed at the top of their game. Our record label hadn't even batted an eye. They didn't care one way or another who was managing us as long as we were selling albums and making new ones.

I hadn't wanted Emmie working as hard as she had been for so many years so I asked her to hire help. Drake and Shane's sister Natalie had been the perfect answer. She was going to college part-time and wanted a job. It was convenient that she lived on the East Coast because she could help Emmie take care of Drake's needs when it came to America's Rocker. Natalie was smart and efficient. A bonus was that she didn't take crap off of Em, who could easily walk over a person without even realizing it. Emmie called the girl her right arm, not understanding how she had managed so long without her help.

"Rich is here?" I demanded, anger making me tense.

"He's trying to get past the security gate," Jesse told me, already reaching for his keys. When I started to follow him, he shook his head. "No. You are going to stay here. I don't want to take the chance of things getting ugly like they did last month. That's why Em asked me to take care of this."

I grimaced, knowing he was right. In Rich's rage he had done the one thing that would sign his death warrant. He had threatened Emmie. He had taken one menacing step toward her, and I had laid him flat on his back with a punch to his glass jaw. The guys and I had left him lying on the floor in his conference room at his office. That bastard was lucky I hadn't done more than hit him. At that moment I had wanted to tear him apart.

His secretary had called the cops and the police had actually showed up here at the house. Rich had wanted to press charges against me. But when Emmie had told the cops what had really happened, they hadn't tried to arrest me. Instead they had asked if Em wanted to take out a restraining order on Rich. Emmie had and when the tabloids had gotten their hands on that juicy little bit of information all hell had broken lose for Rich.

If Rich was here now, even if he was at the gates that lead into our community he was in violation of the restraining order and could be arrested. But I knew that Emmie didn't want that kind of publicity on our wedding day. That she was asking Jesse to handle it rather than just calling the cops told me that much.

Not long after Jesse had left, Lana and Harper came over to check on me. I was already showered, and had gotten as far as putting on my dress pants. I was walking around with no shirt on which had the girls stopping and gawking at me.

"Nice ink!" Lana exclaimed, stepping closer to get a better look.

I glanced at the new tattoo I had gotten just the night before. I hadn't gotten the tattoo I had wanted when we were staying in Florida the summer Emmie had been pregnant with Mia. Every time I had made plans to go to Miami something had always seemed to come up. But with Emmie away I decided it was now or never.

A heart engulfed in flames on my left pectoral. Inside, in cursive black ink, was fan-favorite lyric from *Ember*, the song I had written for Emmie. It had made it to number one for five consecutive weeks on the Billboard chart. *There's this Ember in my heart that has hold of me and it won't let go...*

"So that's where you and Shane were when I called last night." Harper grinned. "I thought it was him getting the ink though."

I shrugged. "He got some ink too." But I would let Shane show it to her. Just as my ink was a surprise for Em, Shane's was one for Harper.

Drake came out of the bedroom, a towel wrapped around his lean waist. Upon seeing his wife, he seemed to light up from the inside out. "Hey, Angel. Enjoy your time at the Spa?"

"Not as much as I thought I would." Lana walked into Drake's waiting arms. "I missed you."

"So, did you get new ink too?" Harper asked, bending to pick up Mia who was holding her arms out to the beautiful violet-eyed woman.

"I didn't leave the house. Someone had to watch Mia." And he never missed out on a chance to spend time with Mia. Drake brushed a tender kiss over Lana's lips and stepped back. "I have to get dressed, Angel. No, don't come in here. Shane's in the shower."

"But..." Lana's bottom lip stuck out in a small pout. "I haven't seen you in two days."

Drake laughed, something he did a lot more often these days. I wasn't ever going to get tired of hearing it. There had been too many years when Drake hadn't even smiled, let alone laughed. "Five more minutes isn't going to be the end of the world, Angel." But he ended up rushing to get dressed and was back within two minutes, fingers combing his long dark hair.

"Let's take Mia for a walk on the beach," Lana suggested, taking the baby from Harper and reaching for Drake's hand. "I'm sure she is getting restless stuck in here."

"She could use some fresh air." I brushed a kiss over Mia's cheek as they passed. "Bye, baby doll."

"Bye, Da-da." Mia waved her chubby little fingers then blew me a kiss over Lana's shoulder before the door shut behind them.

Left alone with Harper I turned to face the girl I was sure would end up my sister-in-law eventually. "How is Emmie?"

Harper grinned, violet eyes lighting up. "Well …"

"Is it that bad?" Was Emmie having second thoughts?

"No, it's not bad at all." Harper rushed to assure me, seeing how pale my face suddenly got. "That's not what I meant, silly. It's just that Em is a control freak and all the caterers are running for their lives because someone forgot to include those little franks in a blanket that you love so much."

I breathed a sigh of relief. "Oh, okay."

"Relax, big guy. Emmie isn't going anywhere. All she could talk about for the last two days was you and how much she couldn't wait to be your wife."

I knew I had a goofy grin on my face. "Good."

When Shane came out, he took one look at Harper and they disappeared into the bedroom again. The violet eyes Drake had sketched up for him looked so alluringly real and was now inked into his chest. Harper had been both speechless and teary eyed. When I started hearing Shane's groans, I grabbed my shirt and headed for the door. Yeah, that wasn't awkward at all! I liked Harper a lot; she wasn't like Shane's normal type. Listening while the two of them fucked in the guesthouse bedroom made me feel all kinds of wrong.

The tent was still being set up, along with chairs and a few tables that would be groaning under the weight of food later. I stood at the back of the tent watching everyone hard at work. I wanted to make Emmie's day a little easier if possible and was willing to step in if needed. But knowing Emmie, she wouldn't stop rushing around, even if she had a hundred people to help her.

I could hear Mia laughing farther down the beach and the sounds of Drake laughing in between making growling monster sounds. I grinned to myself at the sound of such happiness coming from two people that I loved so much.

"Well if it isn't the luckiest bastard on the face of the planet," a deep, lazy voice called from behind me.

I turned my head to find Axton walking toward me. He was dressed up in new jeans and a burgundy red shirt with a leather jacket. Most of his tattoos were covered up, but his facial piercings were still in. I raised a brow at how put together my friend was today. The last time I had talked to him he had been the drunkest I ever remembered him being. I hadn't really thought about the reasons for it until Drake, and then Shane, had told me what was going on.

Dallas Bradshaw, Lana and Harper's old roommate and quite possible the hottest blonde on the planet, had broken up with Axton right after New Year's. I wasn't sure what had happened. The first time I had seen those two together I thought that it was really a perfect match. Truthfully, and I had told Emmie once after meeting the girl, I thought Dallas was Emmie's doppelganger in personality and spirit.

Axton had been seriously infatuated with Dallas from what I had seen the few times that we went out together. But it was something that only those closest to him could see. Ax put on a front that made people think that he didn't have a care in the world. That he was some rich, arrogant, asshole rock star that didn't take life seriously. It was true that Axton lived hard and played harder, just as it was true that the guy could be a total bastard. But he was also the most sensitive and kindhearted guy I knew.

"You're early," I commented as I turned to shake my friend's hand. There was still at least an hour before the guests would be allowed in. Security at the gates of our community was tight today. Emmie wanted to make sure that our wedding was kept private and quiet, not wanting our big day to be the product of the media circus.

Harper, who worked for *American Rocker*, was also our photographer today. Emmie had asked her to do a story on it for the magazine so that Demon's Wings' fans would get the true story of our wedding day. Harper's boss was the happiest man in the media world right now. The exclusive was going to mean big things for his magazine.

Axton shrugged his lean shoulders, thrusting his hands into his jeans' pockets. "Figured I would come and give you guys a hand…" He glanced around the tent. "Where is everyone?"

I grimaced. "She's not coming man."

Axton's jaw clenched. "Who?" he asked the question casually enough, but even now he cast his eyes around for her.

"Dallas. She isn't coming. Natalie and Linc arrived last night, but Dallas was too busy."

"What the fuck!" he exploded. "She can't be bothered to come to her friend's wedding?"

I sighed. "Axton she's running on fumes right now. Nursing school is hard shit. From what Emmie and the others tell me, she barely has time to sleep because she's studying hard."

My friend frowned. "Nursing school? When did she start nursing school? Fuck, when did she even get accepted?" He whispered the last question, his eyes stormy.

"Last month sometime. I only remember that because Emmie sent her some kind of big basket as a congratulation." I shrugged. "Apparently getting into the nursing school Dallas got into is a big deal. They only take a perfect score on the entrance exam."

"That must have been why she came by…" Axton muttered to himself, turning away from me and walking away as if he had completely forgotten I was standing there.

--

With ten minutes to go before Emmie was supposed to walk down the aisle I was starting to shake. My heart was racing, my palms sweating, and my brain tormenting me. Was this what Drake had felt as he had waited to marry Lana back in December?

The Rocker That Holds Her

I was so ready for this thing to be over.

I stood at the back of the tent. After getting ready, I had dressed Mia and then handed her back over to Lana and Harper so that they could fix the little girl's hair. As efficient as I might have been with dressing my child, I still had no clue how to handle her hair other than brushing it each day.

Nearly every seat in the tent was already occupied. We hadn't invited more than twenty people that were in our immediate family. The members of OtherWorld were all in attendance. Liam was the only one to bring a guest, other than Devlin, who brought his ten-year-old son Harris that looked just like the long-haired, dark-eyed drummer.

I had always liked Liam's sister, Marissa. When I had first met her she had been a very sick, very skinny teenager. I couldn't honestly remember what cancer Marissa had had at the time, but I knew that if Liam hadn't been able to afford the treatment she needed back then she would have definitely died. To look at her now you would never have known that she had once been so close to death. With her waist-long, dark chestnut hair, that porcelain complexion, and the curves that only a real man could handle, she was like some ancient goddess come to life.

Marissa was the kind of woman a man had to stop and catch his breath when he looked at her. Even women tended to be overcome by her sheer beauty, and not just because of the way she looked. There was something about her that called to others' souls and made them want to be close to her.

She stood between her bother and Wroth, who was Liam's cousin—but for some reason not Marissa's—as she greeted me with a bright smile. "I'm so happy for you and Em!" she exclaimed softly giving me a gentle hug.

I gave her a careful squeeze in return before she pulled back. "Thanks, Rissa."

She stepped back between her brother and Wroth, who shook my hand. Wroth had a tendency to intimidate everyone around him, even those that knew him better than I did. Having been in the Marines and serving three years in Afghanistan, he had demons that I didn't think I ever wanted in my head.

"You seem to be doing a lot better than Dray did a few months ago," Liam observed. I noticed his eyes were glassy and wondered if weed was the only thing he was high on today. Last fall it had been cocaine that he was playing around with.

Of the five members of OtherWorld, Liam was the only one I couldn't bring myself to like. When Drake had been drinking so much, he and Liam had been friends, if only because they both needed to self-medicate to sleep at night. I couldn't even stand to be around the man when he was high like he was now.

I grimaced. "I'm shaking in my boots, man. Good thing I'm only ever doing this once. I don't think I could handle this shit again."

I talked with them for a few more minutes before my band brothers came out of the house. The three left to find their seats right beside of Lana's father, Cole Steel. I still couldn't wrap my head around the fact that Lana had been fathered by that particular rocker.

I waited for my brothers to join me. A glance at my watch told me that I had less than five minutes before my life changed forever. Drake reached me first, and gave me a hard hug. He slapped me on the back. I clenched my jaw, determined not to tear up.

Shane was next, squeezing the air out of me before stepping back and giving me a serious look. "You're one lucky fucker, Nik. She's so beautiful. Wait until you see her."

I swallowed hard but didn't say a word. I wasn't sure if I could have gotten anything out even if I tried. Jesse stopped beside of me and I expected him to hug me or even punch me. But he just gave me a nod, his throat seeming to work with emotion, and the four of us headed to the front of the tent and the arbor where the minister was waiting on us.

My hands started to tremble and I clenched them into fists at my side. To look at me you would think I was in pain standing there with a grim look on my face that belied my true feelings. "Deep breaths," Drake muttered beside of me with a hint of a grin. "It helps man. Trust me."

I nodded, taking his advice as I sucked in a deep calming breath. As I released it, letting go of some of my tension, music began to play. It wasn't the traditional music that most brides walked down the aisle to, but we weren't the traditional bride and groom so why should anything else be?

Emmie had left the choosing of the music to me, and at first I had thought that writing a song would be the best thing. But after trying to find the words that described how I felt about Emmie, trying to put those words to music without breaking down and crying like a little girl, I had given up and set out to find something else. It had been by happenstance that I heard The Goo Goo Dolls' song, *Come*

The Rocker That Holds Her

To Me on the radio on my way home with Mia one evening. I had stopped in the middle of late evening traffic as soon as the words of the song had registered in my mind. It had been as if the song was written with me and Emmie in mind.

Now, as the song began to play through the speakers set up discreetly in the tent, I raised my eyes to wait for my bride to come to me.

Harper, followed by Lana, came down the aisle looking beautiful as ever in the pink and black dresses Emmie and Layla had commissioned a new designer to make for the bridesmaids. The pink silk trimmed in black lace ended at their knees, and they wore black ballet slippers. It was simple, classy, and so my Emmie's style.

Next came Layla, her dress just a little longer than the other two girls. She caught my eye and gave me a wink as she walked toward us. For some reason that calmed me more than the deep breath had and I smiled back at her.

Lucy appeared at the end of the aisle with Mia right beside of her. Both girls wore silver dresses that looked like they should have had wings sprouting from their backs. Lucy held onto a little basket and walked patiently beside of her *cousin* as Mia took pink and black rose petals from the basket and carefully dropped them along the path they walked.

When the girls reached us, Mia gave me one of her chubby fingered waves before running toward Drake, whom she had attached herself to more so than the other two. Drake swung Mia up into his arms and gave her a smack of a kiss on the cheek, telling her what a good job she had done.

Meanwhile, I was anxiously watching the end of the aisle. Emmie hadn't appeared yet and I was starting to shake all over again. But even as I started to take a step to go in search of her, my beautiful bride appeared at the back of the tent.

My breath froze in my throat. My heart, having been racing away in my chest, completely stopped as the most exquisitely beautiful woman came into my line of vision. Everyone around us disappeared. All I could see was Emmie. Her silky auburn hair was hanging down around her shoulders and was delicately curled to perfection. The dress she had finally found after months of searching was off the shoulders with a neckline that dipped and showed off her breasts in an alluringly sexy way. Black lace accented her waist, drawing my eyes to how tightly the cloth clung to her. The skirt was what I had heard Layla call a mermaid tail.

Maybe it was just me, but I was sure I was marrying the most beautiful creature I had ever set eyes on. Fuck, I was a lucky bastard!

Even though I hadn't wanted to cry and had promised myself that I wouldn't, I felt the tears sting my eyes. Emotion clogged my throat at how beautiful she was and I swallowed hard so that I could breathe once more.

Emmie took two steps down the aisle. That's as far as she got before I found myself moving toward her, not even realizing I was doing so until I heard Shane asking me where I was going. Emmie stopped, watching me with eyes filled with her own happy tears as I closed the distance between us.

I was going to ruin her makeup, but I didn't give a fuck. As soon as I reached her I wrapped my arms around her waist and lowered my head. I needed her kiss more than I needed air. She made a little whimpering sound in the back of her throat as we tasted each other for the first time in two days.

When I finally had the sense to pull back, I found her smiling up at me. "I think that was supposed to wait until after the minister pronounced us man and wife," she whispered.

I dropped a kiss on the end of her nose. "I couldn't wait that long."

"Do you think we should get married now?" she asked with a grin that melted my heart and made me wonder why I had been so anxious in the first place.

"Only if you kiss me again." My lips where already teasing her own. "And tell me that you love me."

She dropped her bouquet, delicate pink and black roses falling to the sand, as she cupped my face with both hands and kissed me. Even as her lips caressed my own, I heard her whisper the words I would never tire of hearing.

"I love you, Nik."

Coming In 2014

The Rockers' Babies

The Rocker That Wants Me

Reece—Book 2 (Title To Be Announced)

Playlist

Come To Me by The Goo Goo Dolls

Warrior by Beth Crowley

Hell Is For Children by Halestorm

Wish You Never Met Me by Papa Roach

Not Strong Enough by Apocalyptica ft. Brent Smith

In The End by Black Veil Brides

Mine Would Be You by Blake Shelton

Lego House by Ed Sheeran

This I Love by Guns N' Roses

Love All Night by Joshua Adams

Save You by Kelly Clarkson

Still Into You by Paramore

Stay by Safety Suit

Simple Man (Acoustic Version) by Shinedown

Miracle by Shinedown

We Fall Apart by We As Human

You Can Follow Terri Anne

Twitter @ writerchicTAB

Facebook @ facebook.com/writerchic27

terriannebrowning.com

Don't forget to leave a review!

The Rocker That Holds Her

The Rocker That Holds Her

The Rocker That Holds Her

Made in the USA
Charleston, SC
22 February 2014